RETRIBUTION

Wanda Dyson

ISBN-13: 978-1499543520
ISBN-10: 1499543522

Cover Design: Daysong Graphic & Web Design

DEDICATION

To Shannon Marchese, who started me on this
journey with JJ and Zoe.

And to all the fans that wanted the journey to go on.

ACKNOWLEDGMENTS

I want to thank Bonnie Calhoun and Miralee Ferrell for being the right push at the right time for the right reasons.

i

Sunday

PROLOGUE

Sunday pm, Maryland

Lights off, Ian eased his car into the woods near the State Park and cut the engine. Even here, in the middle of nowhere, he listened for the sounds that would indicate a bullet aimed at his head. All he heard were frogs, crickets, and the far-off hoot of an owl.

Assured they were alone, he turned to face the woman in the passenger seat and took her hand in his. "I need you to trust me on this. We can go far away where they'll never find us. Build a life together. You know if we stay here, he'll eventually find out and then he'll kill us."

She slowly shook her head. "We'd never get away, Ian. You know that."

Ian Tummely knew the moment he first set eyes on her that he was inviting trouble. He wasn't looking for a relation-ship and in fact, it was the worst possible time with the worst possible woman. Every instinct told him to stay as far away from her as he could. Instead, he bought her a drink and then asked her out to dinner and fell in love with her over steak and lobster.

"Do you love me?" he asked her.

"You know I do."

"If you love me, go away with me. We can be together and no one will know where we are. No one will find us. We'll be safe."

She chewed on her bottom lip.

Waiting for her answer, he almost held his breath. What if she said no? What If she didn't love him as much as he loved her? What if?

He'd never met a woman like her; graceful, sweet, funny. Too gentle for the man who used and abused her, and kept her under a tight rein. For him, it was all about control, about owning her. Ian just wanted to spend his life with her. Surely she could see that.

"What if he finds out?"

Ian leaned over and kissed her softly. "He won't. I promise."

Finally, she nodded. "Okay." She took a deep breath. "Okay. I trust you."

Grinning, Ian felt like shouting with joy. "I'll start making plans We'll go to one of the islands in the Caribbean. Or maybe South America. Give me a week. Maybe two."

Panic shot across her face and she grabbed his hand, squeezing hard. "No. If we do this, we need to do this now. The longer we take, the more time we give him to find out. We need to go tomorrow."

"Tomorrow. Just walk away tomorrow?" He let the idea saturate and the longer it did, the more he saw the wisdom of it. "You're right. Tomorrow."

"What time do I meet you?"

"Be at the airport by six. We'll catch the first flight south." He wanted to laugh out loud as he pulled her into a hug. "You won't regret this. I'll spend my life making you happy."

So what if she was the girlfriend of a drug dealer and he was an undercover cop sent to infiltrate and bring down her boyfriend?

He was about to spend the rest of his life with the woman he loved and nothing else mattered.

*

Roland Hayes was one of the most feared men in the dark underbelly of the city and he didn't get there by being soft. Or forgiving. He surrounded himself with the toughest killers he could hire and he had his hands in everything that would make him money—legal and illegal. It didn't matter to him as long as it was profitable. And if someone—anyone—interfered in his business, he removed them. And they were rarely seen again.

"Did you convince him?" he asked as he sliced into the succulent filet and slid it through the dark wine sauce.

"Of course. Tomorrow morning. Just as planned." She took a sip of wine and set her glass down on the white linen tablecloth. "You're going to a great deal of trouble for one lousy undercover cop."

"Oh, this is about far more than Ian Tummely. Far, far more."

"Care to share?"

He smiled in the way a cat does when it knows the mouse has given up and accepts death. "There's a homicide cop. I'm going to make sure he dies, doing his job, and no one will ever connect it to me."

Her eyes widened ever so slightly. "Investigating Ian's death."

"Yes," he replied softly, his thoughts already far ahead to the moment when he read in the paper that his target was dead.

"Now I understand."

He reached up, gently touching the patch he wore over his missing eye. "No, you really don't."

*

The next morning, Ian arrived at the airport a few minutes before six and headed for the lounge.

By six-thirty, he was dead.

Monday

CHAPTER 1

Monday am, Maryland

The explosion had nearly taken the stately two story stone structure to the ground.

Zoe Shefford, bride-to-be, stood in front of the Pine Lodge Country Club building, staring in near disbelief. In ten days, she would be marrying the love of her life and after their vows, planned on coming here for the reception.

So much for that plan.

There was nothing but rubble. Smoke, debris, and rubble.

Now what? Crying wouldn't solve a thing but it sure felt like the right answer at that moment.

"Miss Shefford!"

Zoe turned to see Monica Gerling half-walking, half-jogging across the parking lot in a pair of impossibly high heeled shoes that didn't look substantial enough to hold together under the stress.

"I'm so sorry, Miss Shefford," she said breathlessly. "I was going to call you this morning to let you know about this but there's just so much to handle."

Zoe glanced back over at the ruins. "I can see that."

"I'm terribly sorry. I know your wedding is in less than

two weeks..."

"Ten days."

"And I don't know how you're going to find another venue at this late date..."

"Neither do I." This place had, in fact, been her last choice since both Emerald House and the Marriott had been booked solid.

"I have a check here refunding your deposit. I know it's very little consolation at the moment, but I do wish you the best."

Zoe took the check and folded it in half. "What happened here?"

"Oh, it's just dreadful. They think it was a gas leak or something. Perhaps one of the cooks didn't shut off all the stoves properly. The fire marshal is investigating." She was practically wringing her hands as she rushed the words out. "It's just dreadful

Zoe took one last look at the building as if somehow it was going to re-build itself right in front of her. No such luck. "Well, I better find something else as fast as possible."

"Good luck."

"Thanks." Zoe climbed into her car. "I don't need luck," she said to herself. "I need a miracle."

She sat there for a long moment just staring at the destruction. Once upon a time, she had been a renown psychic, called upon by law enforcement agencies all over the country. Now, she couldn't even see trouble coming with a pair of binoculars. *Okay, Lord, I renounced all that but couldn't you have warned me somehow?*

Finally, she pushed aside the self-pity and pulled out her phone. Time to let JJ in on the good news. Let him stress right along with her. It rang three times before he picked it up.

"I'm in a meeting, can I call you back?"

"The country club blew up. I'm hunting a new location for our reception. Call me when you have a few minutes."

"Will do."

"Love—"but he was gone before she could finish. She tossed the phone down on the console and fastened her seat belt. Now what? Twice she and JJ had planned their wedding and twice, something had interfered. This time, she was going to make sure they got married if she had to bring a pastor at gun point and hold the reception at a local sub shop.

Her phone started playing a jaunty tune, letting her know who the caller was. "Hey Mom."

"I'm running late, I'm sorry. I should be there in ten minutes."

Zoe winced. She hadn't even thought to call her mom. "You can forget it. The building burned down."

Her mother laughed. "Funny. Seriously, I'll be there as fast as I can."

"Seriously, Mom. I'm sitting here in the parking lot looking at a demolished building and a check refunding my deposit in my purse."

Silence.

"Mom?"

"You're not joking."

"I wish I were."

"What are you going to do now?"

"Start calling every venue again and see if there have been any cancellations."

"Oh, Zoe. This is just heartbreaking. What did JJ say?"

"Something along the lines of 'I'm in a meeting, can I call you back?'"

"I just heard on the radio. One of their undercover agents was found murdered at the airport. I bet you anything they've called him in on the case."

Probably. If it was high profile, JJ usually ended up leading the investigation. "Mom, maybe I'm not supposed to marry JJ. Maybe all these delays and problems are because the Lord is trying to tell me no."

"I don't believe that for a second. Ask a hundred brides if every single thing went perfect on their wedding day. Two may say yes and that's because they were too starry-eyed to notice what didn't go right."

Zoe leaned back against the seat. "Mom, there's a difference between the wrong cake being delivered, the flowers coming in the wrong color, or a bridesmaid ripping her dress going down the aisle—"

She glanced back over at the pile of rubble. "—and this."

*

Detective JJ Johnson picked up his coffee mug and took a long swallow. He felt bad for cutting Zoe off, but he had a room full of law enforcement officers looking at him to lead the investigation and issue orders, and listening to every word he said. "How soon will we have the airport security tapes?"

"Within the hour," Matt Casto replied as he leaned against the wall, arms folded across his chest.

JJ was surprised Matt could even concentrate. He and his wife, Paula, were expecting their first child any day now. After two miscarriages, Paula had finally carried to full term and Matt was on pins and needles to welcome his first child—a boy—into the world. JJ was pretty sure Matt had already bought every sports item the kid would need through high school. Matt would be in serious trouble if the kid ended up hating sports and took up the flute instead.

"What about the phone records?" JJ asked, looking around at the team he'd assembled mere hours ago.

Gerry Otis lifted his hand a few inches. "On it."

JJ was barely in the door this morning when Chief Harris had done his usual gruff and bark, tossing JJ the file saying little more than, "One of our guys was murdered. Find the killer. Now."

JJ wanted to take it as a compliment that Harris didn't waste time with details because he trusted JJ to know his job and do it well. But Harris was the same way with everyone and if you failed, you were out. The fact that JJ had survived more than twelve years on the job was a testament to his abilities. And those abilities had attracted attention from far more prestigious law enforcement agencies, but in the end, JJ stayed with the Monroe County Sherriff's Department.

Matt pushed off the wall. "Ian's former partner and best friend wants to talk to you."

JJ wanted to shove it aside but he knew how he'd feel if Matt were murdered. Nothing and no one would shove him aside and keep him from helping find the killer. Sighing, he asked, "Where is he?"

"He's been hovering around out there ever since word came in that his partner had been killed."

Matt left the office and returned a few minutes later with Doug Carroll, a tall, almost anorexic-thin police officer with dark brown hair and brown eyes.

JJ set his drink aside and propped his elbows on his desk. "First off, I'm sorry about your partner."

"Thanks." He stared down into his coffee cup, hands trembling ever so slightly. JJ's heart went out to him.

"How long had you known Ian?"

Doug took a deep breath. "About eight years. We went through the academy together. Were partners more years than not. Basically, he was my best friend. And I want to know who killed him."

"We all do and we're working on that. What can you tell me about the assignment he was on?"

Doug slowly dropped into a nearby chair. "You probably know more than I do. I wasn't with him on this assignment. I know he was infiltrating a gang known for drugs and prostitution. There was word on the street that some punk named Roland Hayes was putting a new drug on the street, something called Rose, and it's extremely deadly. Ian was sent in to find out exactly what Hayes was doing and where this Rose was being manufactured. That's about all I know."

"Roland Hayes," JJ replied in low voice. "Never heard of him."

"He's names been floating around for about five years."

JJ shook his head, clearing his thoughts. "When was the last time you spoke to Ian?"   .

"Late last night. He called me on a burner phone. Said that he just wanted to touch base."

"Anything about that call strike you as strange? Off? Out of character for him?"

Doug fell silent, staring at the floor. Slowly he lifted his head. "If you're going to try and tell me that Ian turned, you're wrong."

JJ lifted a hand. "I'm not saying that at all. Never crossed my mind. Ian has an excellent rep. I'm wondering if he knew someone had discovered he was undercover. Maybe he suspected they were on to him. That sort of thing."

Doug took a sip of his coffee. "It's not like him to reach out to me at all when he's undercover. I thought it odd that he called."

"And he never said anything about the case?"

Doug shook his head. "Not a word. Just said he wanted to check in, was I okay, he was fine, everything was going good, looking forward to a vacation when this was over, he'd talk to me soon."

"Did he say anything that might have been a message in disguise?"

Again, Doug shook his head. "Nothing. The call barely lasted five minutes."

JJ leaned back in his chair and picked up his coffee mug. Another dead-end.

Doug leaned forward. "Maybe there *was* something."

"Such as?" Matt asked before JJ could swallow his drink and ask himself.

"He asked me if I was interested in going to Cozumel this year for vacation. He said maybe we should go there, that he heard it was nice."

"What's odd about that?"

"He and I were in Cozumel two years ago on vacation."

JJ glanced up at Matt who didn't need to be told to look into tickets to Cozumel. "I'm on it."

"What?" Doug asked.

"One of the questions I've had," JJ replied, "is why was

Ian at the airport to begin with?"

"You think he was at the airport to catch a plane?" Doug jerked to his feet. "Ian was a good cop. He wouldn't just run out in the middle of a case. If he was at the airport, he was still on the job."

"That's what we need to determine."

Matt hurried into the room and tossed a paper at JJ. "Ian had booked a flight for two to Cozumel."

"Who was the other passenger?"

"*Mrs.* Ian Tummely."

"Ian was married?" JJ asked Doug. "I didn't see that in his file."

Doug shook his head, looking a bit stunned. "He wasn't married."

"Then who was the woman he was about to go to Cozumel with?"

"I don't know." Doug sank back down in the chair.

"Whoever she was," Matt interjected. "She never got on that flight."

JJ stared at the printout. "How do we know that? She would have had to actually fly with her real name."

"Because only two tickets were purchased at the last minute," Matt replied. "All the other tickets were purchased in advance and all those tickets checked in."

"Doug, thanks for your help."

The officer leaned forward. "I need to stay involved. Give me something to do. Don't shut me out."

"You're a cop. You know how this works."

"I'm asking for a favor. Please. I won't get in the way and I might notice something amiss faster than your team."

JJ leaned back in his chair, linking his fingers behind his head. "Matt, take Doug and I want you to check out both were Ian lives and where he was staying while undercover. Find me something.

Matt nodded and headed for the door. "Right."

Doug smiled as he stood up. "Thanks." Then he followed Matt from the office.

"Gerry, you're working on the phone records?"

"Yep."

"He had a burner phone. See what you can find."

"We didn't issue it to him."

"I don't care."

"Right."

JJ was about to give out another set of orders when Marsha Olsen came running in with a set of DVD's. "I have the airport security tapes as well as the tapes around the lounge."

"Any cameras in the lounge itself?"

She shook her head. "Sorry." She held the disks out to him. "You want or shall I?"

"Go for it. Let me know if you find anything at all."

"Okie-dokie."

As soon as his teams were out chasing leads, JJ started putting what he had on the white board along with a picture of Ian. Why was he at the airport? Who was he meeting? Did she kill him or was it someone else? If she didn't, where was she?

He knew it was far too early in the investigation to have many answers but it didn't stop him from writing a ton of questions on the board.

*

Zoe stood on the platform, trying not to cry as the seamstress fluttered about, making apologies and blaming her assistants. The white and gold satin with lace sleeves and Swarovski crystals on the bodice and train had been custom made, but today, it didn't fit.

"This is crazy. A week ago, it fit perfectly just a bit long. Now it's too big. Explain this to me."

"Maybe you've lost weight," the seamstress offered.

"Not an ounce," Zoe replied through gritted teeth. She turned to her best friend, Daria, who was sprawled on the bridal salon's white tufted sofa, texting on her phone. Daria had colored her hair almost white blond this week and tipped the edges with burgundy. After going through so many hair styles and colors with Daria, she wasn't even sure she could recall what Daria's real hair color was. "First the country club, now this. I've got a bad feeling."

Daria didn't even look up. "You're nuts. You're about to marry the man of your dreams, after two foiled attempts and the reception site blows up. It happens. It is not a sign that your wedding is doomed."

"Are you going to text your salon or talk to me?"

"At the moment, handle salon business. Heidi texted me to tell me that Mrs. Snide, I mean Tide, came in today for a trim and doesn't like how much Heidi took off and wants a discount on her haircut."

"So?"

"Mrs. Tide comes in every six months and pulls the same thing each and every time. I think she frequents other salons in between, hitting us all up for discounts on her haircuts."

The seamstress twirled her finger and Zoe obediently turned. "Is she poor or something?"

"On the contrary. Very rich. Just very stingy. Never tips the shampoo girl and gives maybe a dollar or two to the stylist."

"What are you going to do?" Zoe asked.

"I told Heidi to comp Mrs. Tide and to explain that since she has used every stylist I have and has not been happy with any of them, it's best she not return until I get new stylists."

Zoe laughed. "And I'm sure you'll call her when you get a new stylist."

"Oh, of course." Daria waved a hand through the air. "Would I do otherwise?" She glanced up from her cell phone and her face softened. "Oh, Zoe. You look like a dream."

"Yeah?"

"That is just gorgeous. I'm glad JJ saw the other dress and you had this one made. It's far and away the most beautiful thing I've ever seen. Okay, it's a little big, but that can be fixed. Don't stress it."

Zoe ran her hand over the skirt, fingering the soft material. "I just wish I felt better about this wedding."

Daria picked up her phone as it buzzed. "Are you still on that track? The wedding is going to happen, it's going to be wonderful, and who cares where the reception is held."

"I have to find *some* place for the reception, Daria. Do you have any idea how hard this is going to be? I've already called six places and nothing."

Daria tapped out a response to someone and then tipped her head to one side and stared up at Zoe. "We will find you the perfect place and you will wonder why you ever stressed about the country club."

"I'm thinking that maybe I shouldn't marry JJ."

Daria rolled her eyes. "Zoe, this is wedding jitters talking. You love JJ. He loves you. Even more, he adores you. You are going to marry that man, so quit with the negatives. That's my job and I don't like you horning in on my territory."

Zoe debated holding her thoughts to herself but she just couldn't. The feelings were just too strong. "Daria, I'm telling you, I have this sense of impending doom and I don't want to ignore it."

Daria tossed her phone down and turned all her attention on Zoe. "What kind of doom?"

"I don't know. Just this awful feeling in the pit of my stomach and it won't go away. I really do think I need to reconsider marrying JJ."

"Have you considered that the sense of doom has nothing to do with JJ?"

"Yes, and I know that it has *everything* to do with him." She gently touched the lace cuff at her wrist then looked at her reflection in one of the many full length mirrors surrounding her. She looked breathtaking and she knew it. She just didn't think JJ was the man who was supposed to see her walking down the aisle in this dress. "I'm not wrong, Daria, and it's breaking my heart."

"Are you actually considering ending it with JJ?"

Zoe tore her gaze from the mirrors to look over at Daria.

"Yes."

CHAPTER 2

JJ paced the conference room as Marsha gave her update to the team. He wished he could say that it was all nervous energy because a fellow officer had been murdered, but that wouldn't be true. Something was going on with Zoe and he couldn't quite figure it out. He'd called her back, only to find himself going to voicemail. He asked her to call him back. Three hours later and she hadn't. That wasn't like her at all.

"At 5:47, Ian arrived at the airport and went directly to the lounge on the lower level. Just as he approaches the entrance, he meets up with this woman—" Marsha hit the remote in her hand and a photo enlarged on the screen. "who then joins him in the lounge. At 6:18, she exits the lounge and heads to airport security." The picture changed to a shot taken at the security checkpoint. "She goes through security here, showing ID has one EmmaLeigh McLeod. She is twenty-six-years old, never married, works at a sporting goods store in the mall."

JJ stared at the screen. "Any criminal background? Why would she be meeting Ian?"

Marsha smiled. "Two years ago, she was known to be dating—drum roll please—Roland Kent Hayes. She was arrested on drug possession charges along with Hayes in a bust. She claimed Hayes must have put the drugs in her purse because she wasn't involved in drugs. Never had been. Hayes, of course, denied knowing the drugs were there. Her purse, her drugs. He was known for drugs, she had a clean record. He walked; she got three years' probation. He had a better attorney, for sure

"Let's see," Matt chimed in. "Ian is undercover, infiltrating Hayes's operation. He shows up at the airport and meets a woman who is a known associate of Hayes and ends up dead a few minutes later. Coincidence?"

"And pigs fly." JJ picked up his coffee mug, found it empty and set it back down. "But we need to connect her to Hayes now, not two or three years ago."

Gerry leaned forward, his bald head catching a bit of the lights overhead. "Hayes started calling the MacLeod woman about three weeks ago and the calls have been getting more and more frequent. He spoke to her every night for the four nights leading up to this morning."

JJ's nose picked up the odor of burnt coffee which distracted him for a moment. He saw that the empty coffee pot was still on the burner. "Someone get that coffee pot." Two men moved to take care of while JJ turned his attention back to his team. "So, either Hayes found out she and Ian were seeing each other and got jealous, or he found out Ian was a cop and used her to get close enough to kill him."

"I think it plays that he told her to get close to Ian and then kill him," Doug Carroll responded from his place at the table. "Where did she go after she killed Ian?"

"We have her boarding a plane to Fairbanks."

"Alaska?" JJ asked.

Marsha nodded, glancing back down at the file on the table. "Her parents are deceased, but she has a brother who owns and operates a hunting lodge in a remote area of northwest Alaska. It's assumed that's where she's heading."

"Why?" Matt asked. "Why run to Alaska of all places?"

"Because the remote areas of Alaska have little or no law enforcement to track her down." JJ tossed his empty can in the nearest trash bin. "Did anyone talk to the lounge worker?"

Marsha looked over at Harry who looked at his notes. "Guy's name is Chip March, he's a college student, said Ian and the girl came in, Ian ordered coffee for them both, they chatted for a couple of minutes there at the server bar and then Ian went over to a sofa and began working on his laptop. The girl went to the ladies room. That's when Chip decided to go out for a cigarette and didn't see anything else until he came back in ten or fifteen minutes later."

"Where's Ian's laptop?" JJ asked, looking around the room.

No one spoke.

"Find it," he ordered. "It should have been with him when the ambulance gathered up his things."

Wayne rushed from the room.

The phone rang and everyone stared at JJ. He reached over and picked It up. "Yes, sir. No, sir. We're working this as fast as we can, Sir. I'll keep you posted."

He hung up. "As usual, Harris is breathing fire. Matt, what did you find at Ian's apartment?"

"At his residence, nothing, but that was to be expected. At his undercover apartment, signs of a woman's presence— lipstick on a glass in the sink, an extra toothbrush in the bathroom, but nothing to the woman's identity. We can only assume at this point." His phone chirped and he yanked it out to look at it, then the tension drained from his shoulders and he set the phone aside. Obviously, it wasn't Paula letting him know she was in labor. "I did find indications that someone broke in and tossed the place. It's possible that she, or Hayes, had someone go in there and makes sure there was nothing there that would give us a name."

JJ's phone rang and he glanced at the caller, then stood up. "Stay on it and keep me posted." He walked out into the hall as he answered. "Zoe, you got my message."

"Sorry, I had a dress fitting, so this is the first chance I've had to get back to you. How's your day going?"

"Probably as bad as yours. How's your hunt for a new reception location?"

"Dead-ends on all fronts."

"We could skip the reception and just go straight to the honeymoon." He walked into his office and shut the door behind him. When he was met by only silence, he said, "Is everything okay?"

"Are you serious? The country club blew up, my wedding dress has suddenly grown two sizes, I still haven't finished about a hundred other things and everyone's telling me not to stress. Does that sound okay to you?"

"No. I've just never known you to go off the rails like this before." He could practically hear her hissing on the other end of the phone. "I'm sorry, Zoe. I didn't mean to say the wrong thing."

"Don't worry about it. Look I have to go. We'll talk later."

"Okay," he said and realized she had already hung up. He stared at the phone for a long second and then shook his head. Women. Even someone as level-headed as Zoe was entitled to a bad attitude day. Thankfully, she didn't have them often.

Matt stuck his head in the office. "Coroner called. He's done with the autopsy."

"Drug overdose?"

"Yep. Rose. In a deadly cocktail with heroin in the mix."

"Well, that just connected Hayes to the murder, just in case that was in question."

"Can we talk?" Matt stepped into the office.

"Close the door and have a seat." JJ dropped down in his chair and wished he had a power drink handy. He could use the energy boost.

Matt shut the door, walked over and pulled a Red Bull out of his coat pocket. "Thought you might be ready for this."

"Did I ever mention you're my favorite?"

Matt laughed as he sat down. "If the team ever found out that was my secret, they'd have cases of the stuff under their desk."

"Worth considering." JJ cracked a smile as he popped open the can. "So what's on your mind?"

"You okay with the way Carroll is insinuating himself into the investigation?"

JJ shrugged. "Can't say that I'm thrilled, but the truth is, if something happened and you were killed, I'd be all over the investigation, regardless of who was running it. So, I get where the guy is coming from."

"He lost his best friend. That has to be tough."

"It does. Wouldn't want to be in his shoes. And it's not like he's interfering. He just wants to know what's happening. I can live with that."

Matt leaned back in his chair. "True enough. Besides, if he starts tripping on your feet, you'll set him straight nice enough."

JJ laughed. "And pigs fly. He'll find himself locked out of the building, not just the investigation. And while all this is amusing to speculate on, what did you really come in to talk about?"

Matt winced. "Am I that obvious?"

"Not at all. But I know you better than anyone else."

"Truth is, I don't have to be good at algebra to put two and two together. Someone has to go to Alaska and bring our Miss MacLeod back in handcuffs. Please don't send me."

"I wasn't going to. I'm thinking I'll go."

"You? What about Zoe?"

"I'm only going to be gone a day or two. She'll probably be glad to have me out of her hair."

Matt snorted. "After all this time and you still don't understand women. She's going crazy with wedding plans. You're supposed to be hovering nearby to take all the flack when she needs to unload all the stress."

"She called a few minutes ago. The reception building blew up, her dress is now too big and she's not happy."

"Real bad time for you to leave town. Real bad."

"Zoe's not like most women, Matt. You know that. She's solid. Dependable. Good head on her shoulders." He shook his head. "Who am I kidding? She's going to go ballistic."

"Yep."

"She is going to hate this and make no bones about it."

"Yep."

"She may even throw me out of her house."

"Yep." Matt stood up and stretched. "Right after she tells you that if you go, she'll never forgive you."

*

Monday pm, Maryland

He was surprised when Zoe called him and suggested they just meet at Yancy's for dinner. Then again, after the stress of the day, she probably just wanted to talk about options. He could do that. And then drop the bomb about the trip to Alaska after he'd solved her problems.

Yancy's was a small restaurant downtown that specialized in charcoal grilled steaks although Zoe usually went for the fish. It was upscale in atmosphere—white linen on the tables, lights dimmed, wait staff in black, but was downhome in price—a couple easily having a wonderful dinner for less than fifty bucks. It was one of JJ's favorite restaurants so he never said no when Zoe suggested it.

He arrived a few minutes late and Zoe was already at the table. She was quiet and distracted when he joined her, but he chalked it up to the country club blowing up. When he reached down to kiss her, she just offered her cheek. His internal alarm bells started softly ringing.

"You okay?" He eased down in his chair, picking up his napkin and shaking it out. "Scratch that question. Of course not."

"I'm fine." She turned her attention to the waitress, ordered her dinner and then waited for JJ to do the same. After the waitress left, she fidgeted with her napkin. "How's the investigation going?"

He wasn't ready to get into that discussion but wasn't sure

how to delay it now that she'd brought it up. "Slow but sure."

Zoe picked up her water glass. "Well, I'm sure you'll solve it soon. Any word on Paula?"

She was calm, almost serene. Too much so. JJ decided to follow her lead and since she dropped the subject of the investigation, he did too.

"Nothing yet. Matt's still on pins and needles."

"I know they're both anxious for that baby to be born."

When she fell quiet, he tried again to probe into her day. "I take it we still don't have a reception site."

"Nope."

"Any prospects?"

"Nope."

Finally, he leaned back in his chair and took a deep breath. "Are you angry with me about something?"

"No, of course not."

Zoe declined dessert and coffee. JJ took the hint and declined as well, just asking for the check. It wasn't until he walked her to her car that she finally started to talk.

"I think maybe we should postpone the wedding."

JJ took a step back, shoving his hands in his pockets. Now he could hear the warning bells loud and clear. It sparked a bit of temper. "Could you explain because this sounds a little like a brush off but it's been a long time since a woman dumped me so I'm not sure if I'm hearing right."

"I'm not dumping you. I'm just not sure we should get married."

"Let me make sure I heard this right. In one breath, you say postpone the wedding and in the next, we shouldn't get married at all. You're not ending the relationship but you don't want to get married. Do I have that right?"

"JJ, I can't explain. I just need some time to think."

"Okay, so I should go away while you re-think getting married. I call that a brush off. Now why don't you tell me what led to this."

Zoe leaned back against her car, fiddling with her keys. "I can't explain. Nerves. Bad feelings. Every time we get close to the altar, something goes wrong. I'm just wondering if we're making a mistake."

JJ knew that Matt would be whispering in his ear—*"be cool, dude, it's just wedding jitters"*—but it didn't feel like wedding jitters to him at all. "I see. Well, I'll make this easy for you. You call me when you make a decision and if I never hear from you again, I'll assume you're moving on with your life."

He turned and walked away, his pride stinging and his ego hurting. She called out to him but he ignored her, climbing into his car and driving away without looking back.

*

Zoe brushed away the tears as she climbed into her car. She and JJ had weathered so much together, surely they'd weather this.

But she couldn't help wondering if she'd just hurt JJ beyond anything they could weather. She hadn't meant to just drop it on him like that. All through dinner she kept trying to think of a way to discuss the whole thing with him but the words just wouldn't come out.

And now she may have just ruined everything.

What was done, was done.

She was almost home when she received a call from her dad. "Hey, Dad."

"You sound miserable."

"I've been in better moods. What's going on?"

"I don't know how serious it is or even if it is serious, but your mom was having some trouble breathing and then just passed out. I called for an ambulance. Can you meet us at the hospital?"

Zoe pulled up to an intersection and quickly pulled a U-turn. "I'm on my way."

"Honey, don't go getting into an accident. She's awake and responding and the EMT's say there's no danger but I want her checked out."

"I agree. I'll meet you there." She disconnected the call

and worked hard at not speeding all the way to the hospital.

Wednesday

Day One

CHAPTER 3

Alaska

JJ set his file down and stared out the window of the plane as it made its approach. The wind whipped and howled and JJ gripped his seat as the bush pilot turned the Cessna 180 almost sideways as they descended over the snow-covered runway.

"It's called crabbing." The pilot, an old man known as Rusty, laughed at JJ. "Trust me, young fella. I been doing this more years than you been alive. Only way to land in this kinda wind."

"Okay."

Rusty kept on grinning. "Most of the time, the wind's blowing near to a cat one hurricane. You don't keep your nose to the wind, it'll flip this plane like a pancake on a hot griddle."

"Uh-huh," was about all JJ could respond with as he gripped the seat even tighter and started to silently pray.

Rusty nudged him with an elbow. "You ever been to Alaska before?"

JJ shook his head. "No, first time." *And last.*

"She's beautiful, but she's deadly. This ain't the lower 48 and you best keep your mind on that every minute."

JJ let the man's words slide away. He didn't plan on being here long enough to find out how deadly it was. He would pick up his prisoner and be back on a flight to the lower forty-eight by tonight. At least, that was the plan. Either way, he didn't plan on staying any longer than he had to.

He glanced at Doug in the seat behind him. He looked a little green. "You okay, Carroll?"

"Right as rain, Sir."

And pigs fly.

JJ had planned on coming alone but as soon as Harris ordered JJ to take someone with him, Carroll had actually begged to be allowed to come. Picturing himself in Carroll's shoes, JJ had agreed. As long as the man didn't start acting like a cowboy, it would be fine.

At the very last second, Rusty straightened the plane, the wheels hit the pavement, and JJ started breathing again. Rusty cackled again, obviously getting some enjoyment out of JJ's discomfort.

As he climbed out of the little bush plane the cold hit him like baseball bat, stealing his breath away. *This was Spring?* JJ zipped his coat up and reached for his gloves.

"Best put on a hat, son. It's about thirty below out here today. Don't want to get hypothermic first day here."

JJ didn't have a hat. But rather than admit it, he just walked as briskly as he could to what was supposed to be the terminal. It was more of a metal shed. But it was warm inside and JJ embraced it with a deep sigh.

There were only a few people in the terminal. A woman behind a counter, taping away on a computer, a man pouring a cup of coffee over in the corner, and the man JJ was there to meet.

The town's one and only police officer was sprawled in one of the chairs, legs extended and crossed at the ankle, a coffee cupped between his hands, hat on the seat beside him.

He stood up as JJ unzipped his coat.

"Detective Johnson? I'm Ivan. We talked on the phone."

JJ shook his hand. "Pleasure." He waved toward Doug who was shivering behind him. "Corporal Doug Carroll. Do you have my prisoner?"

Ivan shook Doug's hand as he answered JJ's question. "No. Checked on her. She's there at her brother's lodge. We can head out there now and pick her up."

"How do you know she didn't run the minute she saw you?"

Ivan set his hat, something furry with ear flaps. "I know her brother, Detective. And I know her from her yearly visits here. She's used to me stopping in there to check on things. And where could she run?"

One thing JJ had found out quickly trying to make travel arrangements to get here—there were no roads in or out. Bush plane was the only means of travel unless you were stupid enough to want to travel hundreds of miles with a snow machine or a sled team. JJ wasn't up for either of those.

"You don't have any warmer clothes?" Ivan asked.

"I thought it was Spring here."

"The calendar says it is in the lower forty-eight. We don't see that kind of weather up here until June. I've got some suitable clothes for you two at my office. We'll suit you up before we take the snow machines out there to the lodge."

"How far is it?"

"About ten, fifteen miles."

JJ decided that this was his punishment for not telling Zoe that he was taking this trip. Then again, it's not like she'd care much. He stuffed down the little twist in his heart and followed Ivan back out into the cold.

The town of Sonuck, located a little more than five hundred miles northwest of Fairbanks, was a small native village with a population of one hundred and six natives. The people lived off the land—fishing for salmon or hunting moose, bear and caribou—and fighting to survive from one day to the next. Ivan—the town's only law enforcement officer—wasn't even in Sonuck full time. He had some six villages over two hundred square miles to serve and protect.

JJ couldn't even fathom it.

After suiting JJ and Doug up in warmer clothes which included bulky hats with ear flaps, they took snow machines and headed cross county toward The Caribou Lodge and Hunting Center. JJ made the mistake of referring to them as snowmobiles and was quickly corrected by Ivan. "We don't call them snowmobiles up here."

The land was as stark as the moon, just endless white mounds of swirling snow with towering peaks in the distance. There was a raw beauty to it that JJ could appreciate. And he even smiled when he saw a polar bear and her cub loping across the tundra. But the heavy clothing didn't seem to help against the cold wind at all—JJ felt as if he were frozen right down to the marrow in his bones.

Glancing over at Doug, he noted the man looked as miserable as JJ felt. He could relate. This kind of cold was not made for humans. By the time they arrived at the lodge, JJ was fairly sure he'd never be warm again. After stomping the snow from his boots, he followed Ivan into the lodge.

He was expecting something with high ceilings, exposed beams, an oversized fireplace, and groups of people sitting around the fire with cocktails or mugs of hot chocolate. Instead, it looked like something from the late 1800's. There was a large woodstove in the corner that seemed to be putting out more smoke than heat, roughhewn wood floors, low ceilings, and the only occupants were three large men in flannel shirts and lace-up boots sitting around an old scarred table that had seen better days long ago. They all looked up as he walked in and nodded before going back to the bowls of stew. The rich, meaty smell made JJ's stomach growl softly in a plea he ignored.

And the guns. Handguns on the table. Rifles propped up against chairs, walls, and near the door.

JJ leaned toward Ivan. "Shouldn't they have all these guns

locked up?"

Ivan grinned. "This ain't the lower 48. Here, you got a bear pounding on the door, you don't have time to go get your guns out of some gun safe. Life or death is determined in a matter of moments. Seconds. You keep your gun loaded and accessible at all times.

"Hey, Ivan." A young woman stepped into the room with a platter of sandwiches. "I have some Caribou stew on the stove if you need to warm up your gullet." While she resembled the airport picture, it didn't do her justice. She was at least six feet tall with dark brown hair rich with red highlights, a slender nose, and dimples. Her athletic build was attractive but he had a feeling it wasn't acquired in a gym. So why would she let a man like Hayes dominate her life?

Ivan waved her off. "I'm good at the moment."

She set the platter down in front of the men, her smile slowly fading as she picked up on something in Ivan's demeanor. "Ivan? What's wrong?"

"I need to talk to you alone, if I could."

She shrugged. "Sure. Come on in the kitchen."

JJ's gut was all but screaming that something was way off. This woman didn't seem to have a clue and even though she could clearly see JJ's badge at his waist when he unzipped his coat, wasn't upset or nervous. Then again, she wasn't exactly expecting the police to come all the way up here after her.

The kitchen was as stark as the main room. Wood fire stove, sink, butcher block table that served as a work area. This was not a luxury operation.

"Okay, Ivan, who died?" she asked as the kitchen door closed behind them.

"These men are police officers. They're here to take you into custody."

He saw the wariness in her eyes now. "Why?"

"They believe you murdered a cop at the airport."

She merely stared at them all for a long moment and then a slow smile began to spread across her face. "You and your jokes. You had me going there for a minute." She leaned back against the counter and folded her arms. "Now, what is this really about?"

Doug stepped forward, handcuffs in hand. "EmmaLeigh MacLeod, you have the right to remain silent."

All the color drained from her face. "You have to be kidding."

Doug was about to continue but JJ put a hand on his arm. Doug stepped back.

"How did you know Ian Tummely?"

She shook her head, her eyes narrowing a bit as her chin came up. "Oh, no you don't. I've been here, done this and I didn't even care enough to get the t-shirt, so if you have questions for me, we'll wait until I have a lawyer present."

That was all JJ needed to hear. No innocent person called for a lawyer before questioning even began.

JJ nodded toward Ivan. "I have a warrant for your arrest. Ivan has seen it. We're going to be taking you back with us."

She stared hard at them both for a long moment and then nodded. "Fine. Let me get my things and we'll be on our way."

"I'm sorry, Emma," Ivan said softly.

She waved him off. "Not your fault. You were just doing your job. This," she nodded toward JJ and Doug, "is just a witch hunt. You need someone to blame, find someone on probation. Easy-peasy. Case closed. And the truth matters not at all."

*

Maryland

"You should go home, Zoe. You've been here day and night since they brought me into this place."

Zoe turned from the window to look at her mother. Congestive heart failure. The doctor had told them as if he were reporting on a cold—dispassionate, indifferent. Zoe felt the world tilt a little and she hadn't been able to get her feet under her since then. She desperately wanted JJ here, holding her hand through this. More than once, she'd glanced at the door, expecting him to walk through with a bunch of flowers.

"I'm fine," Zoe finally said.

"I'm your mother. Don't try that on me."

"What do you want me to say?" Zoe dropped down in a chair. "Congestive heart failure, Mom. This isn't a joke."

"And I'm not taking it as one but I'm not going to die tomorrow. Something else has you twisted up inside. Do you want to tell me what it is?"

Zoe just sat there for a long moment, staring at the engagement ring JJ had so lovingly put on her finger. "I think I may have really messed up."

"Explain."

She raised her head and looked at her mom, steeling herself against the tears that threatened. "I've been having these really bad feelings about JJ. Twice before we came close to the altar, only to have everything go wrong. Now, here we are just less than two weeks away from trying again and the reception site is destroyed in an explosion. I'm just second-guessing whether I'm supposed to marry JJ or not."

Her mother smiled, shifting in the bed, then reaching for her water cup. "Zoe, I love you dearly but sometimes you make me wonder."

"Meaning?"

"Every bride has doubts and concerns and jitters when they get married. It's not such a stretch that you would have them, too."

"I'm not having wedding jitters, Mom. Truly I'm not. Am I upset about the venue and the gown? Yes. But the bad feeling? That's not jitters."

Her mother sipped some water through the straw, then set the cup down. "And you've prayed about this?"

"Of course. No answer."

"And you've discussed your concerns with JJ?"

"I tried. He got mad and stormed off. Told me to call him when I decided what to do."

Her mom winced. "That doesn't sound good."

Zoe shrugged. "He'll get over it. You know how JJ is."

"He loves you and he may well get over it but I think you might have handled it better. No reason to step on a man's heart if you don't have to."

"The thing is, I really believed that once I told JJ that we should call off the wedding, these bad feelings would stop."

"And?"

"They are much, much worse."

"Still think it's the wedding, then?"

"That's what I can't figure out. If it's not the wedding but it's definitely JJ, then what is it?"

Before her mom could answer, the doctor came in, trailed by two nurses. "Mrs. Shefford. How are we today?"

"I'm fine, not sure about you."

His lips didn't even twitch. "I want to run a couple more tests before I schedule the surgery and then we will set up a regimen for you. And I will expect you to stick to the regimen. Diet, prescriptions, exercise. It all matters."

"I'm well aware of that, Doctor."

Zoe's dad entered the room with a tray that carried coffee and food for him and Zoe. "What did I miss?"

"Not a thing, Keyes" his wife replied. "They want to do a few more tests."

"Better safe than sorry," he replied, setting the tray down. "When do you expect she'll have to have the surgery?"

The doctor stuck his hands in his white coat pockets. "More than likely, day after tomorrow. Unless I find something critical that dictates going in sooner."

*

Alaska

Rusty, the bush pilot, was napping when they arrived back at the make-shift terminal with their prisoner. Ivan woke him up with a hearty shaking. "Get up, you old dog, you got passengers to fly."

Rusty yawned, stretched, and then sat there as if in another world while Ivan and JJ took care of the paperwork for transporting EmmaLeigh MacLeod back to the lower 48. Doug poured two cups of coffee and handed one to Rusty. "This'll get you firing on all cylinders."

"Thanks." Rusty practically drank it all in two swallows. Finally, he stood up and zipped up his coat. "Gonna go get 'er ready, Ivan."

"We'll be out in ten," Ivan replied as he handed JJ another form to sign.

Sure enough, when they all got to the plane, Rusty had released the tie-downs, checked the fuel levels, given the plane the once-over, and had the doors open for them.

EmmaLeigh stood patiently to the side—in handcuffs—watching it all with an expression fairly close to boredom. She had been quiet and complacent since she had been placed in those cuffs and tucked into the sled behind Ivan's snow machine. He wouldn't have been surprised to find out she'd slept the entire way back to the village.

JJ helped EmmaLeigh climb up and into the seat behind the pilot. Since she was cuffed, JJ took care of adjusting her seat belt and making sure she was tucked in safe and sound.

Then Doug climbed up and into the plane. JJ turned to Ivan. "Wait. Your gear. We forgot to take them off."

Ivan merely smiled. "Keep it as a memento of your first trip to the great frontier."

"Thanks." The two men shook hands and then JJ climbed in, taking the seat next to Rusty.

Within minutes, they were in the air. Now that he knew he was headed home, JJ turned his attention to the beauty of the landscape beneath them. Mountains, topped with snow, dominated to the east while flat tundra draped to the west. He saw moose on the edge of the tundra, congregating around a small clump of trees.

Finally, he leaned back and closed his eyes. Might as well catch a quick catnap.

It was the scream that woke him up, but it took a couple minutes to understand what was going on. In spite of being handcuffed, EmmaLeigh had managed to get her arms around Rusty and was grabbing for the yoke. Doug was struggling to pry her hands away. She was screaming at Rusty. Doug was screaming at her. The plane was flying erratic. JJ didn't know who to yell at first.

He reached over and grabbed EmmaLeigh at the wrist and applied pressure. Sure enough, she winced and released the yoke. "Don't!" she screamed. "You don't understand."

Doug tried to raise her arms to remove them from around Rusty. She elbowed him, knocking him back in his seat.

"Stop!" she screamed.

And that's when JJ realized that Rusty wasn't flying the plane. He was unconscious. Taking his hands off EmmaLeigh, he reached for the yoke, but it was too late. He closed his eyes and crossed his arms across his face to protect them. The plane hit the ground with a bone-jarring crush. His head hit something and everything went black.

CHAPTER 4

Maryland

By dinnertime, Zoe had left numerous messages for JJ and he hadn't returned a single call. Some of her messages had been succinct—*"call me"*. Others had been more along the lines of *"I'm sorry I was a jerk—call me."* The latest ones were more like—*"You're scaring me, call me."* Still, no response. Finally, she decided to call Matt. He answered on the second ring.

"Zoe, my favorite blond. How goes it?"

"It would go better if I could get through to JJ."

"Well, I understand that cell reception is really spotty in the part of Alaska, but—"

"Alaska? JJ's in Alaska? What in the world is he doing there?"

"He didn't tell you? He went to pick up a prisoner. He's due back at like three in the morning or something."

Zoe sank down in her favorite chair and breathed a heavy sigh of relief. JJ was okay. He was just out of town and not avoiding her calls.

"I can't believe he didn't tell you. That's so not like him."

"We had a little spat."

"Ah."

"How's Paula?"

There was a bit of a chuckle. "Getting irritated that this baby still isn't here yet. I keep reminding her that her due date is tomorrow and first babies can be late. Or so my mother tells me when I complain to her that Paula is complaining. I wouldn't know, having never given birth."

Zoe laughed as all the tension drained away. "You nut. Tell Paula I'm commiserating with her in my own way."

"Wedding hassles?"

"That's putting it mildly. I'll let you go. I just worried when I couldn't get through to JJ."

"I'm sure he'll call you in the morning. See ya."

"See ya." Zoe hung up her phone, leaned back and closed her eyes. Now that she knew where JJ was, she could go back to worrying about her mom.

*

Alaska

"Detective!"

Deep inside, he could hear a woman calling out him— insistent and harsh. Not Zoe then. She didn't refer to him as detective.

Some other woman then. A stranger. One that needed him. He wanted to respond.

JJ knew he was cold but other than that, he couldn't feel a thing. He had no idea where his arms and legs were. He was aware that flakes of snow were falling on his face and he wanted to brush them away, but his hands weren't working. Floating in that space between aware and unaware, he tried to remember what happened and why he was sprawled out in the snow. It was Spring. Flowers were blooming in his yard, so he couldn't be at home. Was there a late-winter snowstorm he hadn't heard about?

A face appeared above his. "Detective? If you can hear me, blink your eyes."

He told himself to blink and he must have but, once again, he just wasn't sure of anything.

"Good. Just hang in there, okay? I need to check on your partner."

His partner? Matt was here? No. Wait. Not Matt. He was with Paula having their baby. Who else was here? What partner?

He saw a face in his mind but his head was starting to throb, chasing the name away. He felt like this once before— all numb and immobile. When he was shot. And he went into shock. Maybe that's what was happening. He must have been in a car accident and was in shock. No. Not a car accident. A plane? What was he doing in a plane?

Questions bounced, trying to catch the elusive answers he knew were just out of reach.

"Detective?"

She was back and now he could see the trickle of blood running down the side of her face. "Detective? I need you to squeeze my hand. Can you do that?"

He thought he did this time.

"Good. Listen to me. Part of the plane is sitting on top of your legs. I need to try and get it off. Do you understand?"

He licked his lips, pleased that he could do that. "Yes." His voice sounded raspy and thick, but at least he could talk. Another small victory. But a plane was on top of him? Not good.

She lifted her hands in front of his face. They were handcuffed. "I can't do what I need to do with these. Where is the key?"

The sight of the handcuffs jump-started his memories. Alaska. EmmaLeigh MacLeod. The plane. The crash.

He must have been taking too long to answer because she hissed and started digging through his pockets. She found the key and removed the cuffs, tossing them aside.

"You're going to have to help me here, Detective. I can try to lift this piece of metal, but I can't do that and pull you out at the same time. Do you think you can use your arms to slide yourself back?"

"Doug," he managed to whisper.

"Is out cold. You're going to have to do this."

His head was really pounding now, going from a hammer against his skull to a sledgehammer. Still, he slowly eased his elbows back and tried to lift his shoulders. He could see it now. Twisted metal and bits of color. He took a deep breath and readied himself to slide out.

"One. Two."

He tensed as she shuffled her feet and braced against the plane. "Three," she barked and heaved.

Releasing his breath, he pulled. Pain surged up his legs, but he kept sliding back.

"A little more," she said through gritted teeth.

Straining a little more, he heard the sound of a metal on metal screech. He didn't know if he was free or not. Pain sucked him under. He heard himself scream before everything went black again.

*

Maryland

Matt was still studying JJ's case board when Marsha stuck her head in the door. "I thought you'd gone home."

"I'm on my way. Just can't shake the feeling we're missing something."

She strolled into the room and looked at the board. "Like what? We have the airport footage. We know who Ian went into that room with."

"I know but I'd really like it if we had footage of her actually killing him."

Marsha snorted. "As if we could be that lucky."

"First thing in the morning, let's bring that kid back in. I want to talk to him again. He may have seen or noticed something and not realized it."

"Chip Marsh."

"That's him. I want to talk to him."

"Okay. I'll take care of it first thing in the morning."

Matt grabbed his coat. "I'll walk you out."

"Still no word on the baby?"

He flipped off the lights and shut the door. "Not yet. Paula is miserable. Which is making me miserable."

She lighted punched him in the arm. "You ain't seen nothing yet. Wait until it won't let you sleep for more than a couple hours at a time."

*

Alaska

"Why are you going through all of this trouble? They're going to rescue us here shortly."

JJ eased his eyes open and saw Doug sitting cross-legged in front of a fire, his right arm in a make-shift sling, his left foot bare and packed in snow. EmmaLeigh was going through the survival packs from the back of the plane, sorting through what looked to be food rations, first aid kit, tackle box, hatchet, knives, mosquito netting, smoke bombs, snowshoes, a couple sleeping bags, two wool blankets, and several metallic-looking thermal blankets.

"This ain't New York City. It could be hours, it could be days, it could be weeks." She shook out a couple of thermal blankets. "Right now, there's a storm right on top of us and if we don't get prepared, all they're going to find when they get here are four dead bodies. If there's anything left when the bears and wolves get done."

"Funny."

She tilted her head and sent him a scathing look. "In less than an hour, we're going to be sitting in a blizzard with winds that will probably hit somewhere around fifty miles an hour or more. The temperature will drop to below zero. Now, if you want to sit there on your ego, you go right ahead. I happen to want to keep from freezing to death."

"This is all your fault. If you hadn't tried to take over the plane."

EmmaLeigh snorted. "Rusty was unconscious or dead. I was trying to keep us from crashing. You took care of that, didn't you?"

"How was I supposed to know he was sick?"

"Yeah, right."

JJ whistled sharply, cutting through their bickering. They both looked over at him. "Could we cut the accusations and someone tell me what's going on and where we stand?"

EmmaLeigh glared at Doug again and then looked over at JJ. "Rusty is dead. I think he was dead before we hit the ground. Maybe his heart gave out or something. I don't know. We're about to get hit by the storm he was trying to fly around. Your partner has a twisted ankle and a broken arm. You are in worse shape. One of your legs looks to be broken in two, maybe three places, you have a concussion, and there's a deep gash in your thigh and another on your head. I bandaged them, but the wound on your thigh is still seeping. I did the best I could to splint your leg while you were out. Not the best, but it'll do until we can get you to a hospital."

She held up one of the survival packs. "I'm going through these to see what we have and what we can use to stay alive until help comes."

JJ shifted painfully, trying to find a comfortable position and realizing there were none. "So the storm will delay rescue."

"Yes," she replied.

"How long?"

EmmaLeigh blew out a heavy breath. "Off hand? I'd say we have a day or two before they'll be able to get in the air."

JJ closed his eyes. His head felt like it was about to explode. The pain was so sharp he almost wished it would.

"Head hurt?" EmmaLeigh asked.

"Like nothing I've ever felt."

She pulled a small bottle from one of the packs. "I have aspirin. Best I can do."

"I'll take six."

"You'll take four. Aspirin will thin the blood and that's the last thing you're going to need in the middle of a blizzard." She crawled over and helped him, holding the cup of water while he drank the chalky pills down his throat.

Everything hurt. He wasn't sure, but he thought that even his teeth hurt. It was doubtful the aspirin would even touch the pain. "Thanks."

EmmaLeigh had splinted his leg and propped him up against a piece of the fuselage. He had one of those thermal blankets beneath him and another on top of him. Even so, he could feel the temperature dropping as the wind kicked up.

"How do we get shelter?" he asked.

"I found a small tarp in the back of the plane. I'm going to drape it over this piece of the wing. That should cut down on some of the wind. Not perfect but it's the best we got for now."

JJ felt too tired to comment. He closed his eyes. At some point, he needed to set his pain aside and take control of the situation but for the life of him, he couldn't do it right now. Doug was going to have to keep an eye on their prisoner and they both had to pray she kept them alive. No way were they capable of doing it for themselves.

*

When JJ woke up again, the wind was howling, snow was coming down sideways and the three of them were huddled under the make-shift tarp EmmaLeigh had put up over them. There was a small fire but he didn't think it was putting out much in the way of heat. He was cold to the bone.

"You're awake," Doug stated. "Hungry?"

"I don't know," JJ replied honestly. The pain was more pronounced that any possible hunger. "How long have I been out?"

"A couple hours."

EmmaLeigh handed him an energy bar. "That's all there is

at the moment."

JJ didn't open it right away. Instead, he tried to sit up and was surprised at how weak he truly was. And his leg was one mass of burning hot pain in spite of the care EmmaLeigh had administered to it.

"More aspirin?" EmmaLeigh asked.

"Yes, please."

She crawled over to him. "How's the leg?"

"Bad."

She handed him the aspirin and a cup of water. The water was warm and felt almost as good as a hot cup of coffee in the cold. EmmaLeigh had been melting snow for them to drink. Smart lady. She wasn't missing a trick.

The lady in question peeled back the blanket and then the clothing on his leg. "I don't like this."

"What?" Doug asked as he huddled under a blanket.

"The wound. It looks like maybe it's getting worse, not better. But it's too dark to see much."

"We'll check it in the morning," JJ replied. "If we survive the night."

"I can't bring the fire up too much more," EmmaLeigh replied. "We'll either run out of wood or burn down the tarp overhead."

JJ pulled the thin metallic blanket up to his chin. "I know. I've just never known such cold."

EmmaLeigh grabbed one of the wool blankets and tossed it over him. "It isn't as good as the insulator blanket but it might help."

"But you need that."

She shook her head. "I'm far more used to this cold than you are. I'll be fine."

He watched her huddle closer to the fire and felt bad that she was willing to take on more cold so that he could have an extra blanket. "Miss MacLeod, I need you take this blanket back."

She glanced over at him. "There were six insulating blankets and two wool blankets in the survival packs. I have two insulators. I'm not going to freeze to death. When I'm ready to sleep, I'll curl up under those things and be toasty warm."

"Why did you kill Ian?" Doug asked, his blankets up to his chin.

EmmaLeigh didn't even bothering looking at him when she replied, "Until we are with my attorney, I'd appreciate if you stuck to conversation about surviving this plane crash."

Doug leaned forward, his face a mix of determination and anger. "We're in the middle of nowhere. It's just us. I just want to know why you killed my best friend."

"And if I recall, you warned me that anything I say *can*—relevant or not, and anything I say *will*—and you do mean *will*, be used against me."

"And what is that supposed to mean?"

"It means I've been down this road before. I know that even if I just give you my recipe for Caribou Stew, you'll find a way to twist it into a confession of guilt, so thanks, but no thanks."

"An innocent person wouldn't be so guarded."

EmmaLeigh snorted. "In your dreams. An innocent person sits down with the D.A and tries to explain they're innocent and he informs her that he doesn't believe her and her attorney explains that she has two choices. Bankrupt her life to try and pay for a jury trial, or accept a plea deal. Welcome to justice." She raised a stick as if pushing her point home and then tossed it on the fire.

JJ smiled to himself. The girl reminded him of Zoe. The spit and fire of a woman not afraid to stand toe-to-toe with anyone.

His smile faded as he wondered where Zoe was and what she was doing. Had she decided to walk away from their relationship? Or had the whole thing just been a severe case of wedding jitters? How would she react when she found out he'd gone to Alaska? Then again, she might never find out. Unless he died. Then she'd read it in the papers.

His heart twisted again.

For the first time in his life, he'd felt as though he had more than just a woman in his life; he had a partner. She was someone he could share everything with and know that he was loved and accepted. Even when he was wrong, she had a way of making him feel as though he merely stumbled on a learning experience.

And now she was having second thoughts.

That hurt. It hurt like hell. And the only way he knew to deal with it was to try not to think about it anymore than he had to. Keep busy. Stay distracted. And hope for the best.

And could you get any more distracted than being in a plane crash, in the middle of a blizzard, while bringing in a murder suspect?

Munching down on the energy bar was less than satisfying but it was better than nothing. "Is this all we have to eat until they find us?"

EmmaLeigh nodded as she added a little more wood to the fire. "That's all they ever put in those survival kits. They add a tackle box so you can catch fish if you want. And a knife and string if you want to snare a rabbit."

Doug shifted under his blankets. "Ian was a good guy. He didn't deserve to die like that."

The look EmmaLeigh gave him was part compassion and part frustration. "I'm sure he was and I'm sure he didn't. And I sincerely, with every fiber of my being, hope you find his killer. Now, I would appreciate it if you would drop the subject or I can promise you that I will tell my attorney that you badgered me every minute I was in custody."

Whatever Doug was going to say was cut-off by the spine-chilling sound of a wolf howling in the night. And from the sound of it, the wolf wasn't far off.

"Not good," EmmaLeigh said softly. "I would suggest, gentlemen, that you make sure you have your weapons loaded and easy to get to on a moment's notice."

"You think he'd bother us?" JJ asked.

"If he's targeting us, he will most definitely bother us. Let's hope he's tracking a caribou or a moose."

The wolf howled again. Closer this time. JJ eased his Glock out of holster under his arm and set it in his lap.

Thursday

Day Two

CHAPTER 5

Alaska

JJ woke with a start, his hand still gripping his pistol. Slowly, he eased his fingers off his weapon and then flexed his fingers a few times to wake them up.

EmmaLeigh was awake already, building up the small fire. Doug was gazing out at the blowing snow. JJ wasn't sure but he thought it had actually grown colder.

"The wolf still out there?" he asked.

"He's out there," EmmaLeigh replied. "Watching. Trying to decide if we're as helpless as we look."

"Shoot a bullet in his direction and he'll know the answer to that," Doug replied tersely.

"Don't waste your ammunition. We may need every bit of it before this is over." EmmaLeigh tossed a power bar to the two of them. "Breakfast, guys. Enjoy."

Guilt washed over him when he saw the frost in her hair and on her eyebrows. "You should have taken back that extra blanket," he told her, ripping open the power bar.

"I've been colder," she replied as she stood up.

"Where are you going?" Doug asked.

"Nature calls. Don't worry. I'll be back."

JJ looked over at Doug. "I have a problem."

"I'm not going to like this, am I?"

"I'm not exactly in a position to jump up and head out for a nature call. I'm going to need help."

Doug sighed. "I've been dreading going out there but I doubt I could hold it for a couple of days. Might as well take you with me."

With Doug's help, JJ managed, but it took every ounce of energy and determination. By the time they returned, he was sweating from effort and gritting his teeth against the pain. EmmaLeigh shook out his blanket.

Easing down, he quickly covered up against the cold. The worst of the blizzard seemed to be behind them but it was still snowing and the wind was still cutting like a broken glass against their skin. And they might have another day or two of this?

She pushed the blanket off his leg and peeled back the torn clothing. When she winced, JJ asked, "What?"

"It looks red and angry. Off hand, I'd say it's infected." She probed a little more, causing JJ to grit his teeth as beads of sweat popped out on his forehead. "I have a bad feeling that there's still a piece of metal in there. If it's a piece of the top of the plane, it probably has fuel and de-icing chemicals on it."

"Great," JJ replied tightly.

She stared at him. "I have to get it out. You know that."

"I know."

She looked over at Doug. "Do me a favor. Go find the front section of the plane. Dig around. Rusty used to always keep a bottle of Jack under his seat."

"He flew drunk?"

"Never. He didn't drink at all. But he always like to say that Jack once controlled him, now he kept Jack under his feet."

"I don't drink," JJ said through the pain.

"It's not for you to drink. I need it to clean the wound and the knife."

"Got a stick for me to bite down on?" JJ tried to smile but they both knew the pain would be no joke.

Doug returned with a bottle of mouthwash. He looked as if he'd been out rolling in the snow. It was sticking to every part of him. "I didn't find any booze but this has alcohol in it. Will this do?"

"It's going to have to." EmmaLeigh poured a bit on the knife and then put it over the fire. It flared up and burned out.

JJ stared at the knife and knew that hot blade was going to be digging into his leg. He closed his eyes. He'd always thought himself a strong man but right about now, he wanted to curl up and cry like a child. And wouldn't Zoe be giving him a hard time about that?

EmmaLeigh didn't give him any warning and no time to prepare. She had rinsed her fingers in the mouthwash and the minute the liquid on her fingers touched his open wound, he nearly screamed. Instead, he clamped his teeth together, closed his eyes and clenched his fists as she dug out the piece of metal in his leg with the tip of the knife. Then she had the audacity to actually pour a bit of the mouthwash over the wound.

He didn't scream.

He passed out.

*

Maryland

Matt stood outside the interrogation room and watched Chip Marsh for a good ten minutes. Something was nagging at him and it took him that long to finally figure it out. He was far too relaxed. "Marsha, is there anyone in the house that still smokes?"

"Harry, downstairs at the front desk, why?"

"Go borrow his pack, will you? Tell him I just need them for a few minutes."

She gave him a narrowed look but left to get him the cigarettes. When she returned, he stuck them in his pocket and then headed in to talk to Chip.

"Chip, appreciate you coming in and talking to us." Matt shook the young man's hand with a big smile. "As you can imagine, any investigation into the murder of a police officer means every T has to be crossed."

"Don't know what else I can tell you."

Chip was at that thin, gawky stage better suited to sixteen-year-olds. It wasn't particularly attractive on a twenty-three-year-old. His hair was a little too long and he had a habit of constantly pushing it back with his hands as if he wanted to put it in a ponytail. When he wasn't messing with his hair, he was sprawled back in his chair as if he didn't have a care in the world.

"Well, it never hurts to go back over the details, just on the off-chance that there was some little detail that you might have missed."

Chip shrugged. "Okay. Whatever."

Matt pulled out the pack of cigarettes and offered one to Chip. "Smoke?"

Chip shook his head.

"It's okay," Matt assured him. "We smoke in here. No one's going to complain."

The young man shook his head again. "I don't smoke, man."

Matt feigned surprise. "Really?" He set the cigarettes aside and flipped open the file folder on the table. "But you told the police officer that the reason you were not at your station was because you want out for a smoke."

Chip licked his lips and dropped his eyes, obviously scrambling for a plausible explanation. "Um, I just told him that because it sounded better than taking off for some air."

"I see. You went for air." Matt leaned forward. "You want to re-think that story? You see, Chip, you are now obstructing a murder investigation. You lied to a police officer. What else are you hiding? I'm thinking that maybe you want me to arrest you and let you sit in jail for a while. I'm sure you can come up with ten or twenty thousand for bail. Oh, and add another three to five for a good attorney."

Chip wasn't sprawling in his chair anymore. His whole body was as stiff as the expression of panic on his face. "Look, man, I didn't see nothing. I swear."

"Where were you?"

"Outside man, outside. The lady gave me a hundred bucks and told me to go outside for a walk."

Matt pulled out a picture of EmmaLeigh and slid it across the table. "This lady, correct?"

Chip stared at the picture, licked his lips again, and then nodded. "Yeah. That's the lady."

*

Zoe tried JJ's cell for the third time as she sat down in the hospital cafeteria with her father for a bite to eat. "It's still going to voice mail."

"Honey, if he got in at three or four in the morning, he's probably still asleep."

Sighing, she tucked her phone in her pocket. "Maybe you're right."

He used his fork to point to her salad. "Eat."

She tried. She really did. Her father kept pushing her until she ate nearly half of it before he finally raised the white flag. "You aren't eating enough to keep a bird alive. You need your strength, but you're a grown woman and I've never been good at nagging."

"Actually, you're very good at it. Just the right mix of nag and guilt." She wrapped her arm around his waist as they walked back to her mom's room.

"I'm worried about you," he told her.

"I'm worried about mom."

"Don't. She's in good hands and we caught this early."

As they turned down the hall, they saw the doctor running into her mom's room. Zoe felt her heart jump in her chest.

She and her dad looked at each other and then they both rushed forward.

They were stopped at the door by a nurse. "Please stay out in the hall for a few minutes."

"What's happening with my wife?" he demanded.

"Sir, please." The nurse turned pitbull, using her body to push him back out into the hall. "I'm asking you to just stay here and let us work. We'll be with you in a moment."

Zoe grabbed her dad's arm and squeezed lightly. "Come on, Dad. Let them do what they have to do. We need to stay out of the way."

He backed up but she could tell it was taking all he had not to plow through the nurse and get to his wife's side.

It took a moment for Zoe to realize that her cell phone was ringing. She stepped away from her dad to answer it.

"Zoe? Matt. I just got a call from the State Police. JJ's plane didn't make it to Fairbanks."

"Didn't make as in he's delayed?"

"Meaning the plane is lost." She heard a hitch in his voice before he said, "I'm sorry, Zoe. They believe it crashed."

It took a moment for that to move through her brain, shove aside her concern for her mother and take center stage. "And they've started searching, right?"

"No. There's been a storm raging. They can't start searching until it's safe to fly."

Zoe's father touched her arm. She glanced up and nodded. "I have to go right now, Matt. When do you think they will start the search?"

"Another day or two is what they're telling me."

"Please call me if you hear anything. I'm at the hospital with my mom."

She hung up the phone and looked up at her dad. "What?"

"They're taking your mom into surgery now. We're to go with this nurse. She's going to take us up to the waiting room in CCIC."

The waiting room was far better than the one they'd seen

several floors below. This one had a television and a coffee bar, but instead of uncomfortable plastic chairs, this room had leather recliners, a coffee station with varieties of coffee and tea, a snack machine, and a table with three computers and internet connections.

Zoe collapsed into one of the recliners. "How long did they say the surgery might take?"

"Three. Four hours." Her father was perched on the edge of his seat as if he wanted to be ready to jump up and run to his wife's side at a moment's notice. "Your call. Was it JJ?"

She shook her head. "It was Matt. JJ's plane is missing. They think it crashed."

He slowly turned his head and stared at her. "And you're not going crazy?"

"I am inside. My head is spinning so fast I think if I really consider all that's going on, I may splinter into pieces."

"Your mom is going to be fine. If you have to go check on JJ, do it."

"There's nothing I can do, Dad. They can't even start searching for him because of a storm. He could be out there, injured, in pain, slowly dying, and it's because I sent him out there. If I hadn't made him mad, he wouldn't have gone."

"Nonsense. He went because it was his job to go. And you have to have faith that he's going to be fine."

"And you have to have that same faith that mom is going to be fine."

He stiffened and then slowly eased back. "Touché. I'm terrified that your mom is going to be taken from me."

"And I'm terrified I'm going to lose Mom and JJ."

He reached over and took her hand. "And we are not to be terrified. We are supposed to trust the Lord, so why don't we cast our cares upon Him and trust that He's got it all worked out in our favor."

"I don't know if I have the strength at the moment," she said softly.

"I'll pray," he replied. "You just agree with me."

"That I can do."

*

Alaska

JJ woke up to the sound of howling winds and EmmaLeigh and Doug arguing. He wasn't sure which bothered him more.

"With the storm, no one is going to be looking for us. And I don't know if Rusty filed a flight plan or not. He doesn't usually because his flights are short jumps from one village to another. That means, they won't be sure where to start looking when they do start looking."

"They'll have the emergency beacon."

"Maybe. If Rusty got his fixed, but when he flew me in just days before you arrived, he said it was out for repairs."

"So what's your point?"

Cupping her hands, she blew warmth onto them. "I'm telling you that we can't just sit here. We need food."

"I am not giving you a gun, lady."

"Then you go hunt up some Ptarmigans."

"Some what?"

"Exactly, city boy. If we're going to survive, I'm the one that has to keep you both alive. Your Lieutenant is bad shape. He needs protein in his system. Broth."

"Well, let's just order in some chicken soup."

"Ptarmigans are similar to chicken, Corporal."

"Oh."

JJ whistled. It wasn't very loud, but it had the desired effect. They both turned to look at him. "What do you think she's going to do, Carroll? Shoot us? After doing all this to save our lives?"

He turned to EmmaLeigh. "And it's only been what? Thirty hours since we crashed? We still have those protein bars."

"Not good enough. You have an infection running through your body. You're too weak to fight the cold off.

You need more than some energy bar."

Slowly he sat up, trying to show he was stronger than she thought and felt himself wince when the pain shot through from his leg to his brain. "I can handle a couple more hours. Right now, I need warmth more than I need food."

"And hot Ptarmigan broth would help feel all warm and toasty inside."

He pointed to the aspirin bottle at her feet. "And you are as likely to give up on this as a dog is to give up a meaty beef bone."

She shook out four white pills and handed them to him with a cup of water. "I don't plan on losing either of you until we get rescued, especially not to some misplaced male ego."

JJ handed her back the cup. "This has nothing to do with my ego."

"Not yours," she replied drily. "His."

Doug glared at her. "Police simply don't hand over weapons to prisoners and tell them to have a nice day."

"Police don't usually end up in the middle of the Alaska wilderness in a crashed plane and the prisoner being the only person that has any idea at all as to how to survive."

JJ opened one eye. "If the two of you don't stop bickering like a brother and sister, I'm going to separate you and send you to your rooms."

EmmaLeigh smirked as she put a little more wood on the fire. "Bottom line is that it's getting colder and this fire is barely putting out enough heat to keep our core temperatures high enough to prevent hypothermia. A few more hours of this and we're going to be in serious trouble. We need hot protein to warm the inside and while I'm cooking the Ptarmigan, I'm going to peel back the tarp and build up the fire for a while."

She turned and looked at Doug. "And this is non-negotiable if you want to get your Lieutenant home alive."

Doug zipped up his jacket. "Then I'm going with you."

"Have you ever been hunting before?" JJ asked.

"No. Why?"

"Because I have. And if you say one word, just one, that causes her to miss her target, or if you scare away the animals because you are chattering away, I may kill you if she doesn't."

JJ handed her his Glock. "This will do the trick."

"Yes, it will. I won't be long. Stay close to the fire." She threw her blanket on top of him. "And no more aspirin until I get back. You truly can not afford to thin your blood right now."

"I got it, Mom. And I'll be good and not open the door to strangers."

She tipped her head and gave him one of those looks women were famous for. Memories of Zoe giving him those kinds of looks rose up hot and fast and punched him in the gut. He'd been doing his best not to think about her, telling him she was calling off the wedding, but it was always there, hovering just below the pain, ready to swamp him.

He remembered the first time he'd met her. Meeting her was the last thing he'd wanted but she'd been called in by the higher-ups to help him solve a case. She'd walked into his office like a dream in gold and green, pink and yellow; a long full skirt that floated around her like a cloud of flowers, and a pair of delicate pink sandals. It may have taken him months to admit, but she'd walked out of his office that day with his heart in her hands.

What he wouldn't give to have her stick her head inside this makeshift tent, snort in a very ladylike manner, and tell him it was time to come home and get married and buy that house they both liked by the lake, and start a family. He told her once that he wanted four boys. She'd merely raised an eyebrow and told him he'd be happy with what he got.

He didn't doubt that for a second.

But he did doubt his future with her. What if she really didn't want to marry him?

*

Maryland

Matt thanked the State Trooper and dropped the phone back in the cradle.

"Well," Marsha asked, leaning forward.

"They still can't start the search."

She stood up. "This is crazy. We are not going to lose JJ to some snow storm."

"No, we aren't. They know what they're doing. We just have to sit tight and let them handle this."

"Does Zoe know?"

Matt let out a heavy sigh. "Yes. I called her and told her. She's a little preoccupied at the moment with her mom in the hospital, otherwise she'd be pacing this room, insisting we call the FBI, the CIA, Homeland Security, and her friends at the White House."

"She has friends at the White House?"

"I don't know, but it wouldn't surprise me. Where are we with Ian's case?"

"We have phone calls linking Hayes with the MacLeod woman. We have her with Ian, paying off college boy to take a walk, and Ian dead when the kid returns. MacLeod jumps on a plane and takes off for Alaska, and now JJ and Carroll are missing in a snow storm, parts unknown, with said MacLeod, while we sit here and do nothing."

"Funny," Matt replied drily. "Might I remind you that JJ is my best friend and my wife is overdue and stressed about the baby, and I should be home with her, not here worrying about JJ but I am."

Marsha threw up her hands. "I'm sorry. You're right. I'm just at my wits end."

"Join the club. I'd give my right arm to be able to jump on a plane and head for Alaska to look for JJ myself."

"Paula would kill you."

"In a heartbeat."

Matt's cell phone emitted a bright little musical tone and Matt snatched it up. "Paula?" He started pacing, nodding, and muttering a few "uh-huh's" before he finally said, "I'm on my way."

"Paula's having contractions. I gotta go."

Marsha tilted her head. "You're a lot calmer than I thought you'd be."

"She said that the contractions are still very far apart and that I'm not to rush because she doesn't want me in an accident." Matt grabbed his coat. "So, I'll use my siren."

"Matt?"

"What?"

"That's my coat."

He stared down at the jacket and then tossed it to her before grabbing his off the back of his chair. "I'm fine. Really."

He got as far as the door when Marsha called out to him. "Matt?"

"Now what?" he asked, turning to face her.

She held up his car keys. Jingled them. "Need these?"

He stared at her a long moment. "You drive."

"Good idea."

*

Alaska

EmmaLeigh gazed around as she stepped out into the howling wind. Snow wasn't falling as thick but the wind was whipping it up off the ground and obscuring the landscape in gusts and drifts. The plane was in four pieces, nearly buried by the snow. Only the red striped tail section was sticking up like a beacon.

Ducking her head against the wind, she headed for a small patch of scrub and brush about thirty yards away. If there were any Ptarmigan close by, they'd be hunkered down in the brush, trying to stay warm.

She couldn't blame them.

"What do they look like?" Corporal Carroll asked in a near

whisper.

"White. Solid white in a blanket of solid white."

"Then how will you find them?"

"Experience."

"You think they are in that brush?"

"No."

She could hear Carroll huffing and puffing as they struggled to walk in the thick snow. City boy. He wouldn't last five minutes out here on his own.

"Then why are you looking there?"

"Never discount luck."

But sure enough, there wasn't anything in the brush except more snow. Well, it just wasn't her lucky day. She started pushing through the snow toward a grove of trees about a quarter mile away.

"Where are you going now?"

"That grove of willows."

"But that's so far."

She glanced back at him. "I'm sorry. The grocery store was closed."

He just frowned at her, but to give him credit, he stayed with her—still huffing and puffing with exertion.

As she approached the grove, she moved slower, almost stealth-like in her effort to move in closer and not scare the birds away. Unfortunately, she didn't find any Ptarmigan.

She shot a rabbit instead.

Food was food and protein was protein.

"Rabbit? You shot us a rabbit?" JJ eyed the skinned animal with wariness.

"I gather you've never had rabbit." Emma was hammering a piece of metal from the plane into a makeshift pot. It was looking more like a battered wok. "Tastes like chicken."

"Why do people always say things like that? You know, snake, frogs—it all tastes like chicken."

"Easier than forcing you to eat at gunpoint." She filled the pot with snow and put in on the fire, then started cutting the rabbit into smaller pieces.

"Where's the skin?" JJ asked.

"Far from here. Along with anything we aren't going to eat. That blood is going to attract predators for miles, so the further it is from us, the better."

"Understood."

"How are you feeling?"

"Like I've been chopped into pieces and then stuck back together. Everything hurts."

She stirred the meat into the boiling water and then turned her attention to JJ's leg. "It doesn't look much better," she said softly after peeling back the bandage.

"At least it doesn't have bad breath."

"You're strong enough to make jokes. That's good."

"That's because you don't know me. I only joke when I'm feeling bad. The worse I feel, the worse the jokes get."

"I'll keep that in mind," she replied, re-applying the bandage.

Scooting back away from him, she pulled her purse out from under her blanket and dumped the contents out. She sorted through it all until she found what she wanted. "Ah-ha, salt."

Sure enough, she had a handful of salt packets from McDonalds.

"You steal salt?" Carroll asked.

"I save salt instead of throwing it in the trash like most people do when they don't use all the cashier gives them." She broke open some of the packets and poured the salt into the boiling rabbit. "You will thank me later."

*

Maryland

Zoe had gone down to the cafeteria to bring up some food for her father when she saw Matt running down the hall near the emergency room.

"Matt?"

He spun on one foot. "Paula. She's in labor." He held up a small suitcase. "I left it in the car. She needs it."

"What floor are you guys on?"

"Four," he answered breathlessly. "What about you?"

"Seven. Mom's in surgery."

"I'm sorry. I'll check in on you if I have time."

"And I'll check in on you if I have a chance."

He smiled and ran off toward the elevators.

At least someone was about to have good news. She turned back toward the cafeteria and nearly ran over Marsha. "Oh, you startled me. I didn't realize you were here."

"Matt is a basket case. I had to drive them both here. How's your mom?"

"Still in surgery."

"Wait. I thought she wasn't scheduled for surgery for another day or two."

"That's was the plan but something happened and they rushed her into surgery and haven't told us anything."

"Where are you headed?"

"Cafeteria. Dad needs to eat something."

"I'll bet you do, too. Come on." She linked arms with Zoe. "I'll go with you. Matt doesn't need me anymore."

"You don't have better things to do with your time?"

"I'm taking my lunch break here. Then I'll head back to the office."

"How's the investigation going?"

"A lot of questions still unanswered. We're more concerned with JJ's safety at this point."

"Have they started the search yet?"

"Not yet."

"I don't like this, Marsha. He could be seriously injured."

"Matt has been all over them like a bird on a fishing vessel."

Zoe narrowed her eyes as she looked over at Marsha.

Marsha shrugged. "Okay, not the smoothest delivery but

he's been relentless with them."

"But now he's in a birthing room somewhere with Paula."

"That's just a few hours and then trust me, he'll be back on the phone with these guys demanding to know when they're going out." Marsha reached for a salad and put it on her tray. "He knows how worried you are and that you need to be with your mom right now. Matt won't let you down."

"This is Paula's first. This could take days."

Marsha eyed the Jell-o and then passed on by without taking any dessert at all. "Paula wouldn't dare. She knows she has to zip right through this childbirth thing."

"Zip."

Marsha deliberated over the salad dressings. "Zip what?"

"Zip. JJ's dog. The kid next door usually takes care of Zip when JJ's out of town or bogged down at the office on a case. He would have told Josh to take care of Zip up until yesterday morning."

"And the kid wouldn't have noticed that JJ isn't back yet?"

"Maybe. Maybe not." Zoe paid for the food on her tray as well as Marsha's. "Do me a favor. Take this up to my dad in the CICU. I'm going to run down to JJ's and make sure Zip is okay and then I'll be right back."

"Okay."

It took Zoe twenty minutes to get to JJ's townhouse. The tulips were dying but the roses were starting to bud. The grass needed to be mowed. She ran up the sidewalk and let herself into the house. Josh had all the mail and newspapers stacked neatly on the table near the door.

Zip nearly knocked her over when she shut the front door behind her. "Hey, boy. How ya doing?" She scratched him behind the ears. "Let's go see if Josh is taking care of you."

She let Zip out the back door, re-filled the food bowl, and noted that the water bowl had been filled that morning. Josh was still on the job. JJ better give that kid a very special Christmas bonus this year.

She wandered through the living room, watering plants

that probably didn't need it, straightening pictures that weren't really crooked. The pain of missing him swamped over her. She felt the tears welling up.

The front door opened.

"Hello?"

"I'm in here, Josh."

When JJ first met Josh, he was a skinny little kid who loved Zip but could barely summon the strength to hold on to him. Now, he stood nearly as tall as she was. She could see the little boy disappearing and the young man emerging. What was he now? Fifteen?

"Hey, Miss Shefford. I saw your car. Is Mr. J. back?"

"Not yet. Aren't you supposed to be in school?"

"Early release today."

"Oh. Well, Mr. Johnson is delayed in Alaska and it may be a few more days before he gets back. Can you still take care of Zip?"

"Sure. Mr. J. always sends me a text message when he gets back. I figured he was delayed. He's okay, isn't he? I know they have bears in Alaska."

Zoe forced herself to smile. "Of course, he is. No bears to worry about."

Zip barked at the back door and Josh walked over to let the dog back in, saving Zoe.

"Well, you have things well in hand here. I'm going to get back to my mom. If you need me, call me. You have my number."

"Sure, Miss Shefford."

Zoe drove back to the hospital in a fog of worry and heartache. Bears. Wolves. Plane crash. Blizzard. Could it get any worse for JJ? She just wanted him to come home. She wanted to marry the man she loved. She wanted him safe. And she wanted him found.

By the time she arrived back to the waiting room, Marsha was gone and her father was standing at the window, hands clasped behind his back, staring out across the parking lot.

Immediately, she rushed forward. "Dad?"

He turned around. "There you are. Your friend said to tell you that she had to get back to work and would call you later. Nice lady."

"She's a police officer. Dad? What about mom?"

"The doctor just came in. She's fine. She's going to be fine." And then she saw him crack with emotion. The tears began to run down his face and his shoulders shook. "I thought I'd lose her."

"You promise she's okay?"

Hayes Shefford nodded and swiped at his tears. "Double bypass but she came through with flying colors and I can see her in about an hour."

"And they're sure she's fine?"

"Positive."

"Then I have to go to Alaska."

He took her hands and squeezed them. "Of course you do. Where in Alaska do you need to go?"

"Anchorage."

"I'm going to call a friend of mine. He has several corporate jets and has told me more than once that I can use one if I ever needed it. I never have. Until now. It will get your there faster."

"Are you sure?"

"The man would give his right arm to help, believe me. Go. Pack. I'll call you with the details as soon as I talk to him."

"You'll tell mom I love her, won't you?"

"Go. And she'd be telling you the same thing. Go get your man."

*

Alaska

JJ had to admit, the woman had a way with rabbit. Or maybe it was just that hot food tasted so good and went so far toward warming him up. Either way, he finished off two helpings and then slept for a couple hours.

When he woke up, it was dark out. Doug was sleeping. EmmaLeigh was staring at the fire, poking it a little.

"Any more aspirin?" He asked softly so as not to awaken Doug.

"Sure." She shook out four and then handed him a cup of tepid water. "How are you feeling?"

"Worse and better."

She touched his forehead and winced. "You have a fever now. I don't like that."

"I'm not thrilled but I've had fevers before. Is it me or has the snow stopped?"

"The storm is over. The sun will shine tomorrow. They'll start the search."

"So they may find us tomorrow?"

"Needle in a haystack, Lieutenant. But anything is possible. For your sake, I hope they do." She moved his blanket off his leg and peeled back the bandage. He saw it in her eyes.

"What?"

She held the bandage up for him to see. Blood. And pus. "I'm going to clean this out again. It won't be pleasant."

"Nothing about this trip has been so far. No point messing with a perfectly good streak."

When he saw her put snow in the makeshift pot and put it on the fire, he knew he was really going to hate what she was going to do.

She went on to examine the splint and seemed satisfied that the breaks below the knee were still stabilized and the bindings still tight.

"Were you born here in Alaska?" he asked.

She gave him a wary look as she cut strips of bandage from the first aid kit.

"Then talk to me about what color you like. What kind of pie. Anything to keep my mind off the fact that you are about to clean that wound with boiling hot water."

She sighed heavily. "I wasn't born here but I was raised here. My parents were free spirits living in Arizona but they felt civilization was encroaching on their lifestyle so they moved my brother and I to Alaska when I was two. I don't remember Arizona at all."

"It's a lot warmer than Alaska."

She smiled as she dropped the bandage into the boiling water. "True enough."

"So did your parents buy the lodge?"

She shook her head. "They started out homesteading. Sustenance lifestyle. If we didn't grow it, make it, or hunt it, we didn't have it. About six years ago, my parents flew down to Michigan for my uncle's funeral. They were on their way to the airport to fly home when they were hit by an eighteen-wheeler and killed. Driver fell asleep at the wheel and crossed the center line. My parents never knew what hit them, so to speak."

"I'm sorry."

"They faced hypothermia, bears, wolves, snakes, lack of food—one impossible obstacle after another to make a life here and they're killed back in the lower 48 by a driver who fell asleep. I couldn't believe it."

She withdrew the bandage from the water with a stick. "Anyway, my brother and I were given a large settlement—as if that was going to make it easier—and my brother bought the lodge. He'd been working as a hunting guide for years, so it was a natural progression for him."

JJ clenched his teeth as she set the bandage on his leg. "And…you."

"I was just so angry. I travelled for a while. Didn't settle anywhere very long. Ended up working at the sporting goods store, helping people prepare for camping and hiking and rock climbing. I found I liked it and ended up staying."

He knew the heat was helping his leg but it was pure torture.

"Tell me, Lieutenant, how long have you been his partner?" she asked, tipping her head toward Doug Carroll, who was still sleeping, snoring lightly.

"He's not my partner and I've never worked with him before. He wanted to come along on this trip because it was his best friend that was killed. Why?"

She shook her head. "Just conversation."

His instincts rang lightly but just then she wiped another hot bandage across the wound, wiping away seepage and the pain swamped his thoughts.

"Get some rest, Lieutenant. Tomorrow could be a busy day."

Friday

Day Three

CHAPTER 6

Alaska

By the time Zoe packed, got to the airport, waited for the plane to arrive and re-fuel, it was nearly midnight before they took off. She spent the first hour of the flight taking in the luxury of the plane—the soft as silk leather seats, the polished walnut, the thick carpeting. She had been grateful to her father for arranging the flight primarily because she thought it would get her to Anchorage faster. But the moment she sank down into those seats, she realized that she needed this flight for another reason entirely. The steward on the flight showed her the seat was a recliner, served her a cup of hot decaf tea, and turned down the lights. She leaned back, closed her eyes, and let the sheer exhaustion flood over her.

Sure enough, she didn't open her eyes until the steward woke her to tell her that they were getting ready to land in Anchorage.

Stretching, she realized she felt energized and mentally alert for the first time in days.

"What time is it?" she asked the steward.

"Almost three."

Hours to waste before the sun came up and a search could begin.

As if reading her thoughts, the steward said, "There's about sixteen hours of daylight in Alaska now, so plenty of sun to search by."

"Thank you."

She buckled her seatbelt as they began their descent. Sixteen hours of daylight to search with. She liked the idea of that although hopefully they wouldn't need all that time. If they could find him in the first hour or two of searching, she'd be happy.

After departing the plane, she was surprised to see a man standing nearby holding a sign with her name on it. She walked over to him. "I'm Zoe Shefford."

He reminded her of her father—tall, gray, dignified in a comfortable manner, and blue eyes that were as warm as his smile. "My name is Nick, short for Nick, and I will be your driver, personal assistant, and go-to guy for your stay in our city. If you need it, I am the person you need to turn to."

"I need to find my fiancé," she replied with a smile.

"Then let me get you to the State Police Search and Rescue." He took her bag and carried it out to a black limo and popped the trunk with his remote. "Since you will be spending most of your time with State Police, we have taken the liberty of securing you a suite at a hotel nearby."

He opened the back door for her and then placed her luggage in the trunk.

There was orange juice and coffee waiting for her. She reached for the juice first and wasn't surprised to find that it tasted fresh squeezed. Her dad's friend truly knew how to pay her dad back in spades.

Assuming they were going to the hotel first, she was surprised when they pulled up in front of an official looking building with glass doors. "Where are we?" she asked, but Nick had already climbed out of the car.

She asked again when he helped her out of the limo.

"The police know you are coming and there are people

here for you to talk to about the search."

She felt like mountains were being moved for her. And boy was she ever grateful.

"How will I contact you?"

"I'll be here when you need me."

"It could be hours."

"So be it. My orders are to be at your beck and call. When you sleep, I sleep." He nodded toward the doors. "They're waiting on you."

In spite of the hour, she found a conference room full of uniforms waiting for her. They offered her coffee, introduced her to representatives from various search and rescue operations and then brought her up to date.

"First off, we have received no emergency beacon signal from the plane. Second, the pilot did not register a flight plan. Therefore, the search area is over 2 million acres and we have no idea where in all that area they might have gone down. We can assume, from what Ivan told us, Rusty knew the storm was coming in and would have flown east to stay out of it as long as possible. But how far did he get before he went down? We simply don't know."

With each word, Zoe could feel the hopelessness bearing down on her. They didn't have any hope of finding anyone alive.

"So what is the plan from here?"

"We did send out some planes yesterday afternoon as soon as the weather cleared, but they didn't see anything. We've coordinated with some of the local search and rescue teams that operate out in the Denali area and they will out at first light on snow machines. We will have helicopters and planes in the air at first light. Some of the local bush pilots will be helping us as well."

He leaned forward, his elbows on the table. "I know I'm making it sound hopeless but I don't want you to give up hope. We're limited on resources, but it doesn't mean we're not going to put everything we can into this."

There was a knock at the door, someone stuck their head

in and signaled to him. He rose. "Excuse me a minute."

Zoe's cell phone chirped. She pulled it out. It was a text message from her dad.

"U there?"

She typed back. "Y W/SAR"

"Story?"

"Keep hope but hopeless. Massive search, Limited resources."

"Miss Shefford?"

She glanced up to see a man in a Coast Guard uniform standing there. She rose to her feet. "Yes?"

"I doubt you remember me but we met once in Florida. Marathon Key."

She took a sharp breath. "Maizie. Maizie Vandenburg."

He nodded. "Yes. I don't think I'll ever forget that little girl. I can see you haven't forgotten her either."

"You were the one who found her on that raft." She vaguely recalled the red-haired Coast Guard Swimmer who had been given the task of jumping from the helio into the waters of the Atlantic to retrieve the body of the nine-year-old. The child had built a raft and was sailing to the Caribbean to be a pirate. She had been pulled out to sea from her parents private beach and lost for almost a week on a little raft in the hot sun with no food, water, or shelter.

"Too late, unfortunately. I just wanted to say hello. And to tell you that I thought you were amazing that day, talking us right to her even though you were miles away. It was incredible."

"But it didn't do her any good, did it?"

"We were able to bring her home to her parents, Miss Shefford. They had closure. It has to be enough."

He placed his hand on her shoulder. "I want to assure you that we're going to do everything humanly possible to find your fiancé. Don't you dare give up hope."

"I haven't. I won't."

"Why don't I take you to your hotel. Get some sleep. We'll

all start fresh in the morning?"

"I appreciate that but I slept all the way here. I don't think I'd be able to sleep a wink now."

"Then take a shower, get some breakfast and then head back over here around seven. These men haven't slept a wink and they need it even if you don't."

She glanced around and realized they were there out of courtesy for her, not because there was a single thing they could be doing for the next few hours.

Smiling, she picked up her purse. "I have a driver who will take me to my hotel. I'll see you all in a few hours."

*

Maryland

Matt was bleary-eyed when he walked into his office a little after eight. His son, Noah Josiah Casto, had been born just after four in the morning and Matt had been too enamored of his wife and son to sleep a wink all night.

But now it was time to get back to work.

He was pouring himself a cup of coffee when there was a knock on his open door. "Matt?"

Matt stared at the man a long moment before he recognized him. "Adam Healey. What are you doing dressed like a degenerate biker?"

"I've been deep under. This is the first chance I've had to see if I could help with Ian's case. He was a good friend."

Matt shook the officer's hand and then circled the desk to sit. "Doug Carroll's been giving us a hand."

"Who?"

"Doug Carroll. Don't tell me you don't know him."

"Well, of course I know him but I don't know why he'd be helping you. He and Ian hated each other."

Matt pointed to a chair as everything in him stilled and all he could feel was his heartbeat. "Sit. What do you mean hated each other? Carroll said that Ian was his best friend. That Ian called him the night before he was killed. He's wormed his way into this investigation right to flying off to Alaska with JJ."

Adam shook his head. "Ian would never have called that snake. He didn't trust him. Why would he say otherwise? And why would he be helping? Makes no sense."

"I don't know. Start from the beginning. Why didn't Ian trust him?"

Adam shrugged. "Personality clash. Instinct. Doug is sneaky. Or least, he comes across that way. Makes it hard to trust him. It's like he's always lurking around, listening to everyone's conversations."

"Did he go on vacation with Ian to Cozumel?"

"No. Ian and I went to St. Martin's a few years back, but I don't think Ian's ever been to Cozumel, and if he had been, it wasn't with Doug Carroll."

Matt's engines were firing on all cylinders now and he didn't like the sounds he was hearing. "I need to talk to your L.T."

"He's in. Just saw him in his office."

Sure enough, Henry Underwood was combing through some files when Matt knocked on his door. "Henry?"

"Hey, Matt. Come on in. How's the investigation going?"

"That's why I'm here. Did you know Doug Carroll was helping us?"

"Helping you what?"

"Investigate Ian's murder."

"No. He called me Sunday night and told me there had been a death in his family and he needed to take a week off. He's supposed to be in Texas or something."

"He told us that he was Ian's best friend and that they went through Academy together."

Henry shook his head. "No way. They did not go through Academy together and Ian did not care for Doug at all. Doug transferred in from DC Metro about five years ago. Ian was already here. It was gristle and growls between those two practically from the moment they met. I chalked it up to

Doug being such a go-setter and Ian protecting his territory, so to speak. Figured it would settle in time. Never did."

Brow furrowed, he picked up a pencil and let it run through his fingers. "Tried to put them both on a case together once and Ian came back to me and told me that if I forced him to work with Doug, he'd resign. And he meant it. I teamed someone else up with Doug."

He leaned forward and his chair thunked against the desk. "So why is Doug here and what does he hope to accomplish by getting involved?"

"He's not here. He's in Alaska with JJ."

"I thought I heard JJ's plane is missing."

"It is."

"Okay, now I am seriously confused."

Matt stood up. "That makes two of us."

*

Alaska

JJ tried to push his blanket off before he suffocated.

"Oh, no you don't," EmmaLeigh insisted, pushing his blankets back over him. "That's your fever talking. It is not warm enough yet for you to do that."

"Hot."

"I know you are. You're burning up."

JJ opened his eyes and licked his lips. "Thirsty."

"That I can help you with."

She helped him drink nearly a whole cup of cold water before letting him collapse back on his mat. "Fever's worse. Your wound is worse."

"Aspirin."

"No can do, Lieutenant. Wish I could."

"All gone?"

"Everything's gone."

He opened his eyes and stared at her, willing himself to

move through the heavy fog in his brain. "What?"

"Your partner. Carroll. He's gone and took pretty much everything with him."

"Gone?" JJ rose up on one elbow. Sure enough, Doug's spot was empty, blankets and all. EmmaLeigh's pot was missing, as was the survival kit bag she had near the fire with all their supplies. "He took everything?"

"Yep."

"Why?"

"You want my opinion or is that a rhetorical question?"

"Opinion will do."

"We're supposed to die here. He took your gun so that we can't protect ourselves or hunt for food. He took our supplies so that we were helpless. He killed Rusty, although I think that was a bit of miscalculation on his part. I think he merely wanted to make Rusty so drowsy, he'd put the plane down somewhere and then he'd kill us all and fly away."

JJ had to put a great deal of effort into it, but he managed to sit up. And then felt dizzy but ignored it as best he could. "But why?"

"Well, now that's the million dollar question, isn't it? Your Corporal Carroll is dirty, Lieutenant. What I've been trying to figure out since all this started was whether you were, as well. I suppose this answers the question once and for all."

"Dirty? Carroll?"

"I saw him once with Roland Hayes. All buddy-buddy. Roland bragged to me that he had cops in his pocket. Carroll was one of them."

"Which is why you were so nasty to him."

"Was I?" she smiled. "He's lucky that's all I was. If I wasn't so against going to jail for murder, I'd have killed him. I was convinced he was behind me being arrested since the moment he swaggered in spouting off Miranda. I told Ivan, I was just a pawn in the game. Pawns are dispensable."

"Well, it seems you've been miles ahead of me this whole time."

"I wish I could have known whether to trust you or not. I

would've told you what's what."

"I don't know that I would have believed you, anyway, so don't worry about it."

She shrugged. "I get it. And if it's any consolation, you still have that .38 strapped to your ankle. I never let him see that so he didn't know to take it from you. And I hid a few supplies in the kit bag I was using as a pillow, so we are not totally without resources. Just wish I hadn't left the aspirin out in the open but I didn't quite expect this move."

"You are a very remarkable woman, EmmaLeigh MacLeod. If I wasn't already engaged to marry a remarkable woman, I might have to look twice at you."

She laughed softly. "Well, it's a good thing you're getting married because I don't like cops."

The moment sobered quickly, mostly because JJ didn't want to think about Zoe and the possibility that the wedding wouldn't take place. "What do we do now?"

"Our options are somewhat limited. I've been working on them since I woke up. We can stay here like sitting ducks which is exactly what I think he wants us to do. The body requires a lot of protein to fight off cold. Without it, we sit here with no food, hoping to be rescued, fall into hypothermia and die."

"Considering the fact that I'm already hungry, I don't like that one."

"Neither do I, but you asked for all the options. We can try to get down the slope to the tundra. We get out of the snow and we find better shelter, more opportunities for food, and a better chance of surviving long enough to get rescued. The problem with that is two-fold. One—it puts us out in the open where he could shoot us if he thinks we're going to get away, and two—it means me trying to carry you out of here."

"We've done okay so far staying here."

"Sure. We've had hot food to help. Now consider that if I go out there to hunt and Carroll sees that I have a gun, he can shoot me, and leave you here to die alone. He can always tell people that you died from your wounds and I tried to escape, stealing your gun, and he had to kill me. Who's to say otherwise?"

"If he wants us dead, why not just shoot us and go?"

"If we're found shot, it would raise a few questions, don't you think?"

JJ chewed on that for a moment. "If we were able to move further down the mountain, and he shot us, same thing."

"Rescue finds us at the plane shot dead, it raises questions. If we go down to the tundra and he kills us, far more likely bears and wolves will get a good meal but even if they don't, how likely for rescue to find us?"

"Good point. You have been thinking about this."

"I've gone around and around and around every aspect of it. I'd like to live long enough to prove I'm innocent and go home."

"Well, he could have shot us on day one, when rescued, he could have told them that you shot me so he shot you."

"He could have, but he didn't. Only thing I can think of is that the crash threw him off his game. He had to come up with a whole new plan when he couldn't get in the plane and leave."

JJ stared out at the blanket of snow, trying to think, process, and fight off the dizziness at the same time. "If I left it in your hands, what choice would you make?"

"We take our chance on getting to the tundra."

"You can't carry me."

"It won't be easy, but I'd drag you on a makeshift stretcher."

He shook his head and then slowly laid back down, already feeling exhausted and all he'd done was sit up for a couple of minutes. And she was planning to drag him for miles across snow and dirt and rock? It was impossible.

"Maybe they'll find us before we starve or become bear bait."

EmmaLeigh shrugged. "Miracles do happen but keep in mind that they have to search an area that's probably a million and a half to two million square miles in scope with a couple of planes and a couple of helicopters. They have no idea where we are, or when it stopped snowing late yesterday, they'd have made a beeline for us."

JJ flung an arm over his eyes. *Lord, thank you for this woman who is fighting so hard to keep me alive. Keep us both alive. Help her. Help us. Guide the rescuers to us in time. Show us what do to. And Lord, if you could let Zoe know that I love her, I'd appreciate it. She may never hear it from me again.*

They heard a shot in the distance. The sound echoed off the cliffs and through the valleys, distorting its direction.

JJ lifted his arm. "What is he doing?"

"Can't say for sure, but if it were me, I would be killing something and dragging it close by to draw predators to us. He's pinning us in. Bringing every wolf and bear within five miles right to us."

"If he doesn't die out here, I may just have to kill him myself."

There were no more shots. The silence kept them company until EmmaLeigh finally said, "Lieutenant?"

He shifted his arm so that she could see his eyes. "Yeah?"

"I'm going to get us out alive, do you hear me? Don't you go giving up on me."

"I don't give up." *And if that were true, I wouldn't have walked away from Zoe that night. I'd have fought for her. I'd have proven to her that I was worth the risk for life. Instead, I gave up.*

*

Zoe tried to sit in the corner and stay out of the way but it was so hard not to ask questions from time to time. How many helicopters are out there? How far can they see? Do they use binoculars? How long can they stay out before they have to come in and re-fuel? She'd been involved in far too many rescues to not have most of the answers but it helped her from jumping out of her skin.

To give the men credit, they were patient and understanding with her.

She was pouring herself another cup of coffee when one of the State Police officers walked up to her, a sheet of paper in his hand.

"Miss Shefford?"

She couldn't recall his name or rank but he was pretty high up in the chain, she knew that. "Yes?"

"I just got word of your contribution to this endeavor and I wanted to thank you personally. It was very generous."

"I'm sorry. What contribution?"

He handed her the piece of paper. Between her father and his friend, Frank Moss, they'd given the SAR half a million dollars to assist in paying for resources so that it wouldn't come out of the taxpayers' pockets. There was an additional promise for more if it was needed.

Tears welled up in her eyes. She handed him back the notice of funds. "Excuse me a moment."

Rushing off, she nearly ran down the hall to the ladies room where she let herself break down and truly cry for the first time. Her dad hadn't been there for her most of her life but he was determined to make up for it. He knew how much she loved JJ, maybe even more than she realized it herself and he was moving every mountain he could to give Zoe her heart's desire. JJ—alive.

She felt him there with her at that moment. JJ. As if he were standing behind her, wrapping his arms around her, leaning in close. She closed her eyes. "JJ" she whispered. "I don't want to lose you."

She could have sworn she heard him reply, *"Lose me? When pigs fly."*

Zoe emerged from the ladies room about fifteen minutes later, her eyes still red but her heart a little lighter.

At the end of the hall, a man stood, legs slightly apart, arms folded, blond hair glistening from the overhead lights putting a bit of a halo around his head.

Zoe stopped. Took another step and then began to run.

"Donnie!"

"Hey, beautiful. Heard you needed me."

She fell into Donnie Bevere's arms and when he lifted her up, hugging her, swinging her around, she almost broke out in tears again.

When he finally set her down she forced herself to step back. "How did you know? When did you get here? How long are you staying?"

"I called Matt this morning to talk out some plans for JJ's bachelor party and he told me what happened. I got here about ten minutes ago. And I'm staying until our guy is found."

He linked his arm in hers and started walking her back to the conference room. "We got a problem, sweetheart."

"Yeah, JJ's plane crashed."

"And the cop that went with him is dirty. The whole reason he insisted on helping JJ is to make sure that JJ doesn't come back."

She felt an icy chill shoot down her spine. "Why?"

"Matt's still working on the why."

"It isn't bad enough he's out there in the cold with snow and bears and wolves and who knows what injuries, now we have a rogue cop looking to kill him?"

"That's about the gist of it. Sounds like JJ's having a bad day, wouldn't you say?" He pulled the door open to the conference room and stepped in, holding his badge up in the air. "Special Agent Donnie Bevere, FBI. We have a situation."

"Worse than this missing plane?" one of the State Police officers asked.

"Much worse."

*

Doug Carroll had made their decision for them. There was no way they could stay near the plane.

In spite of his best efforts to at least keep EmmaLeigh company while she worked on getting them ready to move out, he felt himself growing weaker and weaker. Finally, he was nodding in and out. When he woke one time, she was gone and he wondered if she'd given up and left him. When he woke again, she was fashioning a makeshift stretcher out of branches and tree limbs and the tarp. He had to give the woman credit—she saw a problem, she fixed it. If he had to be in this situation, he couldn't think of a better person to be on his team. When he woke again, she was taking the plane tie-downs and making a harness for the stretcher.

"I'm still concerned with you trying to pull me in that thing."

She didn't even bother to look over at him as she covered the stretcher with the few blankets they had left to them. "I'm stronger than I look. I can go straight up a rock face with my fingertips. Hauling you isn't going to be any worse than that."

"And I'm heavier than I look. Muscle weighs more."

She gave him a withered look. "Muscle. Right."

"Serious. I work out. Gym. Three, four times a week."

"Lieutenant, I know you are delirious with fever right now so I'm just going to agree with everything you tell me, okay?"

He closed his eyes, a caustic retort on the tip of his tongue.

*

Maryland

Matt combed his fingers through his hair and blew out a frustrated breath. "There has to be a reason for Carroll to want JJ dead. If we go under the assumption that he's dirty, we have to assume someone paid him big money to get JJ to Alaska and into the wilderness."

"It all keeps pointing back to Roland Hayes," Gerry replied. "He's the common denominator in all this."

"But we can't find any connection between Roland Hayes and JJ," Marsha protested. "This is personal. Someone who really hates JJ. Wants him to suffer. Wants him dead, but doesn't want to be directly connected."

"Okay, who is Hayes connected to?" Matt asked.

"That's the problem," Gerry said. "Ian went in to find out and was killed before he could report anything. We have absolutely nothing about Roland Hayes before '09. It's like he's a ghost."

"I don't believe in ghosts. I do, however, believe in men who change their names to hide and reappear somewhere else as someone else."

"You think Roland Hayes is an alias?" Marsha asked.

"It's a possibility. A man like that doesn't get that powerful without showing up on the radar along the way. If there's no record of him as Roland Hayes, there has to be one under a different name."

Matt began to pace. He needed to get to the hospital to bring his wife and son home but hated feeling as though he were abandoning JJ, even for an hour or two. "Did we ever get a picture of Hayes from narcotics?"

"Yeah." Marsha slid it down the table to Matt.

He slid it over to Gerry. "Go see if State will run this through facial recognition for us."

"Don't we have anything we can bring Hayes in on? Maybe we could get some answers if we torture him." Marsha shrugged. "Just saying."

"Ignoring the torture question, we don't have a thing to prove Hayes was anywhere near any of this. Let's find something."

Marsha stood up, gathering up her notes and file folders. "If JJ is out there with this MacLeod woman, who killed Ian for Hayes, and with Carroll, who is also in Hayes's pocket, what chance does JJ have against two killers?"

Matt stared at her a long moment, then turned on his heel and walked out of the office.

CHAPTER 7

Alaska

Zoe was out in the hall, her arms wrapped around her waist when Donnie found her.

"You done playing spectator?"

"What do you mean?"

He tipped his head to the side. "You are Zoe Shefford, *hello*? How many Search and Rescues have you been a part of?"

"Too many."

"And you're content sitting on the sidelines of this one? I don't think so." He took her arm. "Come on. Let's go."

"Where are we going?"

"To get us some proper gear and hire a bush pilot to take us hunting tomorrow."

"Seriously?"

"Seriously. I can't sit around here anymore either."

As they stepped outside, Nick climbed out of the limo and jogged around to open the door for her.

"You have a limo" Donnie asked helping her in.

"Courtesy of JJ's benefactor."

Donnie slipped in beside. "Nice. Always wanted to travel in style."

"Nick," Zoe called out as the driver got behind the wheel and started the limo up. "We need a sporting goods store. A good one."

"Yes, ma'am."

"Where are you staying?" she asked Donnie.

He shrugged. "Haven't even looked yet."

She opened her mouth but Nick spoke up. "I'll take care of that, Miss Shefford."

"Thank you, Nick."

"Man," Donnie stated. "What a life."

"I could get used to it," Zoe replied. "But I don't think it works with a detective's salary."

"Or FBI. Might as well enjoy it while we have it." Donnie shifted in his seat to face her. "Now, you want to tell me what's going on?"

"What are you talking about?"

"I know you well. Something's wrong when I see Zoe Shefford sitting around on her hands, fretting and worrying when the woman I know would be plowing through that group of chiefs up there, barking out orders, elbowing through bureaucracy, and chopping off heads when necessary."

"Not always."

"This is JJ we're talking about."

She turned and gazed out the tinted windows as the car turned a corner and cruised down another street. "JJ and I had a bit of a disagreement before he left. I'd been having all these bad feelings and I thought it was a mistake to go ahead with the wedding until I sorted them out. JJ thought I was dumping him."

"Still think marriage to JJ is a mistake?"

"No. And I'm embarrassed to admit that I thought it at all. Everyone kept telling me that I was reading it all wrong, that I was stressed, that I had wedding jitters. They were more right than wrong. The bad feelings about JJ were right on, but it was this trip to Alaska, not our trip to the altar."

"Hindsight and all that, but JJ loves you."

"I just hope it's not too late. He was truly angry with me."

Donnie laughed. "Darling, it's been what? A week at most? You honestly think JJ's love for you was so shallow that it could die in a week?"

"Okay, you can stop now. I feel stupid enough."

The car pulled to a stop in front of a large store. Nick turned in his seat to look back at Zoe and Donnie. "You'll find anything and everything you want or need here."

He cut the engine and got out to open the door for them but Donnie climbed out and held out his hand to help Zoe. "Sorry, Nick, habit."

"No problem, Sir. I'll be here waiting for you. Would you be wanting dinner reservations?"

"I like the way you think, Nick. Best steak house in the city if you don't mind."

Nick nodded. "I know just the place."

"Do you think you could find us a bush pilot that can take us out tomorrow to help with the search?" Donnie asked as Zoe headed into the store.

Nick nodded again. "What time do you wish to depart in the morning?"

"Seven sounds good."

"I'll take care of it for you, Sir."

"You're a good man to have around, Nick."

"Thank you, Sir."

*

Maryland

Matt stood over the crib, staring down at his son. His son. He couldn't quite believe it was all real but there he was, sleeping peacefully, all wrapped up in a blue blanket.

"He's not going to disappear," Paula said. She was in bed, propped up with pillows, an unread book in her lap.

"I know but I just can't stop looking at him. He really is gorgeous, isn't he?"

Paula laughed. "Yes, Matt. He looks just like you. Now, would you do me a favor?"

"Anything."

"I have your mom cooking everything that can be cooked in the kitchen. My mom is going through the house cleaning what she's already cleaned twice. Both of them are just killing time until Noah wakes up so they can fight over who gets to hold him, bathe him, or rock him. I would actually like to take advantage of them both being here and get a little sleep. Go away and let me rest."

"You're actually trying to get rid of me?"

"Yes. Go away. Go to work."

"You're sure you don't need me to be here?"

She tilted her head and gave him one of those looks that spoke volumes.

"Okay, okay. I'm going back to the office for a few hours but if you need anything, anything at all, call me."

"I will. Go away, Matt."

Half an hour later, Matt walked into the office with a sense of frustration. He felt as though he was just spinning his wheels while the investigation went nowhere.

Most of the staff had gone home but he saw the lights on in JJ's office and in the conference room. He poured himself a cup of coffee and headed in to see if maybe a miracle had occurred while he was gone.

Marsha, Gerry and Wayne were huddled over a file when he walked into the conference room. "Anything?"

"No hits on VICAP but an interesting development."

Pulling out a chair, he sank down into it. "Talk to me."

"A young man just showed up in the morgue. Overdose of Rose." Gerry slid a report across the table to him.

Matt looked at it and then ran his fingers through his hair. "Chip Marsh? Overdose?"

"Nope. Murdered just like Ian."

"But why?" Matt held up his hand. "Don't answer that. It's pretty obvious. Either they killed him because he told us what he knew or they killed him before he could tell us the truth and I'm going to bet he didn't tell us all he knew."

"What else could he possibly have told us?" Gerry asked. "The only thing he had to contribute was who paid him off."

"Whatever it was, it died with him. But he made someone nervous. Tear this young man's life apart. I want everything right down to his twitter account examined. But first, we're going to go rattle a few cages."

Matt snagged his jacket off the back of his chair. "Marsha, concentrate on Marsh for now. Gerry, Wayne, you're with me."

"Where are you going?" Marsha asked.

"Into the lion's den."

*

Alaska

EmmaLeigh huddled close to JJ as darkness fell over the landscape. He was burning hot, tossing and turning, muttering nonsense and flailing against the blankets she'd tucked tight around him.

He needed medical care and he needed it now. Much longer and he'd more than likely lose that leg if not his life. Already, she could smell the stench from the wound when she uncovered it. And it would only get worse with time.

She knew she needed to rest. Tomorrow was going to be a grueling day. Still, she could only stare out at the darkness and wonder where Carroll was and when he'd strike. Her fear had even caused her to smother the fire when it grew dark so as not to make them an even greater target.

She didn't want to die. Not here. Not now. She'd always planned on a long life with kids and grandkids. Now, she wasn't so sure she'd make it another day.

The thought of slipping away in the night crossed her mind. She was, after all, only human, but as much as she might want to, she couldn't bring herself to leave the Lieutenant to die here alone.

For the life of her, she couldn't understand why Roland Hayes had done this to her. After he'd blamed her for the drugs, she'd refused to have anything more to do with him. Nearly two years had gone by and she'd assumed he'd moved on to someone else. But then the calls had started. The veiled threats. The photos in the mail showing her at work, the store, the gym—all so she'd know she was being stalked. Then the threats weren't so veiled at all.

Finally, she'd done the only thing she knew to do. She'd run away, fleeing to the one place she felt safe. Home. Only to have the entire thing follow her.

And now, she was sitting on a mountain range in a couple feet of snow, freezing, hungry, and wondering when the bullet would come that would end her life.

None of this was fair. That was the hardest thing for her to wrap her mind around. It wasn't fair. She had done nothing to deserve this. She'd heard people say many times that life wasn't fair but it didn't seem real. Until now.

Off in the distance, a wolf howled. She sincerely hoped Doug Carroll was shaking in his boots.

Wrapping her arms around her knees, she let her forehead fall forward and closed her eyes. A little bit of rest. Just a little bit.

*

Matt walked into the The Loop, a local restaurant and bar, known to be a frequent hangout for Roland Hayes. He felt like every eye in the place was tracking him as he wove his way through the crowded room. Music blared, hot and heavy, drawing people to move.

He spotted Hayes in the back of the room, sitting in a banquette with two large men—obviously bodyguards—and a beautiful blond who looked as if she would be better suited to a Hollywood soundstage.

Hayes was decked out in solid black—suit, shirt, tie. His watch was black, the two silver rings on his fingers had black stones, and he wore a black stone necklace around his neck. The only color was the silver eye patch, as if he wanted to draw attention to it.

As soon as Matt drew close to the table, the bodyguards stiffened, eyeing him warily. One of them slid his hands under the table, no doubt reaching for his weapon.

Matt eased his coat jacket back so that they could all see the badge clipped to his belt. Hayes leaned back, smiling, throwing his arms along the back of the banquette as if welcoming Matt with open arms.

"Detective. Beautiful evening isn't it?"

Matt placed both hands on the table and leaned in. "I just wanted to let you know that your plan failed. JJ's fine. And your man? Carroll? He's on the run but we'll have him in custody here shortly."

Something flickered in Hayes's one good eye, but the smile remained plastered in place.

"So I wanted to let you know that you should enjoy your last few days of freedom because I'm pretty sure that since Carroll knows what happens when a cop gets placed in general population, he's going to sing loud and long. And when he does, you'll go to prison for a long, long time."

"Detective, I don't know what you're talking about. Who is Carroll? If she's pretty, I might be interested." He laughed at his own joke so his companions laughed along.

"Like I said, Hayes. Enjoy this time while you can. I'm sure that JJ's going to be sitting in the front row when you're sentenced. And he'll be the one laughing. You think?"

Matt saw it then—the tightening of the jaw, the flash of anger in the eyes, the clenching of one hand into a fist—and still the smile never wavered.

"I think if you were half as confident as you try to sound, Detective, you'd be putting me in handcuffs."

Matt stood up straight, letting a slow smile cross his face. "You keep telling yourself that. You see, this is my idea of fun. Knowing you're going to be sweating, waiting for the moment when I come back."

"You got nothing and you'll get nothing, so I'll ask you to leave. You're interfering with my good time."

Matt winked at him, grinning and then turned and walked away. A good bluff could be fun. All he could do now was hope that it worked.

Saturday

Day Four

CHAPTER 8

Alaska

EmmaLeigh woke with a start and her senses went into high alert. Her ears strained to hear in the silence. Her eyes searched through the darkness.

Little by little, with each passing moment, the tension drained from her shoulders. She squinted at her watch, trying to see the time. Four-ten. A little earlier than she'd planned to start but as long as she was awake, there was no point in wasting any more time.

Quietly, she gathered their meager supplies into the emergency bag and set it aside.

"Lieutenant?" she shook him gently.

He didn't even open his eyes. "Yes?"

"We have to go. I'm going to need your help getting you on the stretcher, okay? I can't lift you. If I place it next to you, can you just kind of roll on to it or slide yourself on to it?"

"And pigs fly," he muttered before finally saying. "Yeah. Yeah, I can do this."

But it was hard for him and she knew it. She let him work on slowly moving from his mat to the stretcher while she took down the tarp above them and folded it up to put under his head.

Twenty minutes later, she lifted the head of the stretcher, looped the straps over her shoulders and moved forward. The first few steps were a struggle but once she was in motion, it was a little easier, especially as they began to descend a gentle slope. Several times, she saw dark splashes in the snow and knew that Carroll had killed something and spread the blood around to draw wolves and bears.

She had decided to leave the crash site before dawn in hopes that Doug Carroll would be sleeping and miss them slipping away in the dark.

The plan was still hazy in places but if she could give them a head start, get them below the snow line, onto the tundra, find food, find a way to hide from Carroll—she could figure the rest out as they went along.

She heard the Lieutenant grown from time to time and she felt bad for him but it was going to get far, far worse once they were off the snow and on to rock and gravel, uneven dirt, and slippery mud.

The moon gave her little assistance as she carefully placed one foot in front of the other on the descent, trying hard not to make a misstep and fall.

"EmmaLeigh?" she heard the Lieutenant whisper harshly.

She stopped, kneeling down to hear him better. "Yes?"

"Thirsty."

They could stop here, she could get some of the last of the snow to give him, or they could take their chances further down, hoping to find a stream or creek where the water runs cool and clear.

"I have no water, Lieutenant. I'll find you some as soon as I can."

Silence.

She half turned and realized he'd passed out again. Adjusting the straps on her shoulders, she climbed to her feet and resumed pulling.

The sun tipped over the top of a mountain in the distance,

lighting up the snow topped ridge. Alaska could be harsh, it could be deadly, but she never tired of the beauty.

The low growl raised the hair on the back of her neck and a chill went down her spine. She glanced over and saw the large black wolf, teeth bared, standing just fifty feet away. Slowly, she lowered the stretcher, reaching for the Lieutenants .38 tucked in her waist band.

The last thing she wanted was to fire that gun. With the sun on the rise, the sound ricocheting all over would wake Doug Carroll and send him on the hunt for them.

But she didn't care to get mauled by a wolf, either.

Slipping the straps from her shoulders, she eased back up, bracing her legs in the patchy snow. "You want me, you're gonna die for it, big boy. I'd really prefer if you went looking for rabbits or squirrels or something."

The wolf took a step closer. Then another. The ruff on the back of his neck was up and his lips were curled back.

"Please go away, please go away, please go away."

But the wolf didn't seem inclined to give up the possible lunch he'd felt he'd stumbled upon.

She raised the gun, pointed it at him, still begging him softly to just go away. "If I kill you, there will be no honor in it. No value. You will not feed or clothe me. You will not provide sustenance or warmth to anyone. You may feed a bear or other wolves but it would such a sorry end for a creature as magnificent as you."

He took another two steps forward and she knew and took a deep breath. "Forgive me, wolf. You gave me no choice."

The big black wolf bunched his hindquarters as she aimed and as soon as his front feet left the ground, leaping toward her, she pulled the trigger.

The Lieutenant jumped, his head whipping around. "What?"

"Wolf."

He glanced over, saw it on the ground and sighed. "Oh."

"Oh?" she snarled at him. "Oh? I just had to kill that

animal for no reason whatsoever."

"To protect us."

She tucked the gun in her waistband, slid the straps over her shoulder and lifted the stretcher. "I hate needless death. Senseless."

"He was going to kill us, right?"

She knew he didn't understand and never would. "Yeah. He was going to kill us. The wolf was merely being a wolf. He saw weakness, smelled death, and reacted the only way it knew how."

"Then it wasn't exactly needless. But now, Carroll knows we're on the move."

"Yep, I'm sure he does."

When the Lieutenant didn't answer, she looked back and saw that he was unconscious again.

She had to find him help soon.

*

Zoe climbed up into the back of the plane, letting Donnie take the front seat next to the pilot. As she removed her gloves, she let herself relax for the first time all morning. All through breakfast, Donnie had pushed her to eat her breakfast, reminding her that she would do JJ no good if she was cold and hungry. All she wanted was the time to pass quickly so they could get in the air.

She'd spent most of the night praying and crying, sometimes both at the same time, asking the Lord to give her once more chance with JJ. Now she had circles under her eyes, but she was beyond caring. She just wanted to find JJ. Alive.

Donnie had coordinated with the SAR as to where they would start searching so as not to waste efforts. She just wanted to get in the air and start looking. Finding JJ was all that mattered now.

The whole time the pilot was getting strapped in, checking gauges, talking to the controller, chatting with Donnie, Zoe was in the back, silently begging them to just take off.

Finally, they were on the runway and then in the air, banking to the west, heading northward. She gripped the seat in front of her as she stared out the window, desperately hoping—and expecting—to see JJ down below, waving to her.

She saw bears, moose, caribou, eagles. She saw meadows vibrant with all the colors of the rainbow beneath mountains iced with snow. And rivers as blue as the sky broken from time to time by white rapids. And as wondrous as it all was, she didn't see the one thing she wanted to see.

Up one range and down another. Nothing.

Crisscrossing the tundra. Nothing. She stared until her eyes hurt. Sometimes she used the binoculars, sometimes not. She watched out one side of the plane, Donnie had the other.

"Anything?" she asked about every ten minutes.

"Nothing," Donnie would reply.

Finally, he held up his hand before she could ask. "Nothing and I'll make a deal with you. If I see something, I'll shout it out loud and clear so you'll know, okay?"

Zoe turned and looked back out the window.

"We have to go back in," the pilot informed them.

"No," Zoe said more sharply than she intended. "Not yet."

"Ma'am, as much as I'd like to stay out here, we're low on fuel."

"We can re-fuel and come back?"

"Yes, ma'am. If that's what you want."

"It's what I want."

Donnie shifted in his seat. "We'll get some lunch while he's re-fueling. Give him a chance to grab a bite as well."

She wanted to argue but knew there was no point.

To Donnie's credit, they ate lunch at a small deli just blocks from the airport. It was small, clean, and had a decent menu if you like thick sliced bread baked that morning, slabs of meat and cheese, and a bowls of hot soup. It should have had Zoe's taste buds dancing. It was like sawdust to her. Donnie was shoveling in.

"Donnie, I do want you to know how much I appreciate that you're here and keeping me sane. It can't be easy."

"That's what friends are for. It's not like you haven't kept me from going off the deep end."

A few years back, Donnie's wife, Lizbeth had been kidnapped and Donnie had come very close to diving off the deep end head-first. They'd found Lizbeth, but it had been too late for the child she'd been carrying. At the time, Zoe had concentrated on praying, searching, and keeping Donnie sane and in faith. It should have been easy to allow him to the same for her now.

"Still, I'm not used to feeling needy and weak and I do right now. It isn't sitting well with me." She pushed her plate aside. "I keep thinking about what it's going to feel like if I lose him—knowing that I'd pushed him away. Knowing he died thinking I didn't love him."

Donnie reached across the table and slapped her hand. "Stop. JJ is not going to die out there. And he knows you love him."

"You've seen what it's like out there. Snow and ice and deep crevices that drop hundreds of miles maybe. Bears bigger than a truck. And that's just if he survived the crash itself."

"Will you stop thinking the worst?"

"I can't help it. It's been four days. I heard what those rescuers were saying. Four days out there in that cold, it's unlikely he could have survived. One said it would take a miracle at this point."

"Well then it's a good thing we know just where to go for a miracle or two, isn't it?"

"Donnie…"

He raised his hand again. "When Lisbeth was buried alive and we didn't know where and we were in a race against time to find her, what did you keep telling me?"

"To trust God."

"Take a bit of your own advice, will you?"

*

Matt was surprised to find Marsha in the conference room when he got to work. "What are you doing here on a Saturday?"

"I thought you might need me."

He sat down, rubbing his face with his hands. "I need a lead. I need something that will connect Hayes to Ian's murder and Marsh's murder and JJ's plane crash. I got nothing and it's driving me crazy."

"Before I start, how is your new baby boy?"

"Remarkable."

"Of course he is. Now, do you want some good news?"

"Sure. Can I get a cup of coffee while you tell me?"

Marsha nodded toward the coffee pot. "Help yourself. I just made fresh."

"I knew there was a reason JJ kept your around." He stretched when he stood up and then reached for a coffee mug. "So, what's the news?"

Chip Marsh's best friend came in. He was upset about Chip's death. Wanted to know if it was because he took that money from that guy to take a walk when that cop was killed."

Matt slowly turned around. "He took money from...did you say 'that guy'?"

"I did indeed." She looked down at her notes. "His name is Brian D'Angelo and he's waiting in interrogation one if you want to talk to him."

"I do indeed."

He quickly tossed some cream and coffee into his coffee and rushed out of the room, only to rush back in and take the file Marsha was holding up in the air.

"Thanks."

He found Brian in the interrogation room, looking bored and glancing at his watch. "Sorry for being late."

"No problem, Sir."

Matt dropped the file on the table. "I don't want to keep you long. Just have one major question for you. Are you sure Chip told you that a man paid him off? Not a woman. It was a man?"

"That's what he said. Now, he'd had a few." Brian smiled. "Well, we'd both had a few, but he definitely said that this guy came in and gave him a hundred bucks to take a walk."

"Did he describe the man at all?"

Brian shook his head. "Sorry. He just said something about it being easy money, that's all."

Easy money? It got him killed. Wonder if he'd have thought it as easy money if he'd known he was going to die for it.

SUNDAY

Day Five

Chapter 9

Maryland

Matt stopped at the Java Café across the street from the station on his way in to pick up a large coffee knowing that on a Sunday, no one would be in to make any. He could start a pot when he got in but he needed a caffeine jolt bad and he needed it now.

Everyone had warned him—get sleep now, you won't sleep after the baby is born. How right they were. In spite of the fact that both Paula and her mom did their best to keep Noah's crying to a minimum, it still woke him every three hours.

He backed against the door to push it open and was surprised to find Gerry at his desk, staring at his computer.

"What are you doing here?"

Gerry leaned back in his chair, stretched, then yawned. "Trying to find something on Hayes. I got bupkiss." He lifted an eyebrow. "Bring me one of those?"

"Didn't know you were here or I would have."

"Good thing I made a pot then."

"I'll be in JJ's office if you need me."

"Any word on him?"

"Zoe called last night. Still nothing."

"Well, we can't give up hope. JJ's tough."

"Still hoping and praying, too." Matt stepped into JJ's office and tried to imagine JJ never coming back. It was just too inconceivable. It was even more so at the thought of losing his best friend.

He fired up JJ's computer and then started going through JJ's files, looking for someone who would go this far, and have these kind of resources to kill JJ—other than Hayes.

They were getting nowhere with Hayes but what if it wasn't Hayes at all? What if it were someone else pulling the strings? Maybe someone who has Hayes on a leash?

He went back two years. Then three. Gerry stopped in on his way out to say he was leaving. Marsha stopped in to say she'd come in and asked what she could do.

"Get me something to eat, please?" he asked, never taking his eyes of the computer.

"Preference?"

"Greasy, thick, and full of calories."

"Fat Jakes down the street?"

"Exactly what I was thinking."

He went back four years and was starting on five when Marsha came in and some incredible smells followed her into the room—grease and beef and onions and pickles.

That was enough to tear him away from the computer screen. "You are a life saver."

Marsha leveled him with a look. "Just don't get used to it. Now, what do you need me to do?"

"I'm going back through JJ's old cases and looking for someone who might have been behind all this."

"I thought Hayes was the one we were looking at."

"He is, but it wouldn't hurt to see if there's someone other than Hayes, or someone using Hayes."

"Okay, how much have you done?"

"I've gone back four years, just starting five."

"Eat your lunch. I'll start on five."

"Deal. Then I'll start on six."

They worked until well past dinner time going back twelve

years. He was on the file for a man names Wendell Vernon. It was one of JJ's first cases as a detective. A man was killed outside a bar and two men identified Vernon as the killer, saying that Vernon had gotten into a fight with the man when he refused to pay for the hooker he'd hired.

JJ had gone to arrest him. Vernon had objected, taking a swing at JJ. The two scuffled and Vernon fell against a broken table leg, puncturing his eye.

Leaning back in his chair, Matt smiled. "Gotcha." He spun around in his chair. "Marsha!"

It took her a moment to appear in the doorway. "You called, oh awesome one?"

"Cute. Come look at this mug shot and tell me what you see."

She tilted her head one way and then another. "What am I looking for?"

"Anything familiar."

Suddenly her eyes widened. "Well, well, well."

MONDAY

Day Six

Chapter 10

Alaska

While most people spent their weekend enjoying time with friends and family, EmmaLeigh was dragging the Lieutenant through the snow, down across the shale fields, and onto the tundra. She'd pull for five or six hours, sleep for two or three, pull again for another five or six, sleep again. She thought she'd be able to pick up some speed once they were below the snow line but the rock and shale was far more treacherous. Twice she slipped and fell to one knee before catching herself.

Now her knee hurt and she was walking with a limp.

The Lieutenant was unconscious more and more now. Once he'd groaned after being jarred when she slipped but the rest of the time, she hadn't heard a word out of him. And that worried her. The infection was spreading. His fever was spiking.

And there was nothing she could think to do for him.

Stopping at a small group of boulders near a river, she propped the Lieutenant up and checked on his wound. It smelled worse than it looked.

He barely stirred.

"Lieutenant, I'm going to get us some water. I'll be right back."

He merely looked at her for a moment and then closed his eyes.

Grabbing the two water bottles from the supply bag, she ran down to the river and filled them. She took an extra moment to splash some of the frigid cold water on her face and the back of her neck.

Slightly refreshed, she returned to JJ and sat down next to him. "I have some water. I need you to drink some."

He did, but not much. She took her bandana and washed his face with the frigid cold water, knowing it had to be giving him some relief.

Sitting there, she fought not to get discouraged or overwhelmed. She knew that part of the problem was hunger and fatigue, but she couldn't give in to it.

Digging through the emergency bag, she pulled out what passed for a fishing kit. String and hook. Still, it would work.

For the better part of three hours, she sat by the river and fished. She did manage to catch a small fish she could use for bait, but the larger fish were illusive. Finally, she secured the line with a rock and went to check on the Lieutenant.

He was trying to reach the water bottle. She picked it up, uncapped it and trickled a bit more water down his throat. He needed protein. Setting the water bottle aside she stood up and studied the area. Off in the distance, she saw a brown bear grazing on a slope near the river. That told her there was something on that hill. Like blueberries. They grew wild and plentiful on most of these slopes and the bears loved them. It was a little early in the season for there to be very many, but she'd take what she could find.

There was a problem. The bears would not care to share the berries with her, so she'd have to be extremely careful.

"Lieutenant?"

JJ moaned but didn't open his eyes. She touched his forehead. He was burning up and his lips were cracking. One spot was even bleeding. This was so much worse than she could believe. He was going to die and there wasn't a thing she could do but watch it happen.

She knew he wouldn't hear her but she said it anyway. "I'll be right back."

Moving slowly, she inched her way toward the blueberry field, hoping not to disturb the bear. Taking her time, she never took her eyes off it. At one point, the bear lifted its head and looked over at her, but then went back to eating.

She reached a berry bush and started filling her pocket with berries. As he knelt near another bush, a gunshot blasted into the relative calm and silence on the hillside. The bear roared in anger, turning and running.

Right in her direction.

Another shot kicked up some gravel right behind the bear, angering it further.

Carroll had found them, and now he was trying to get the bear to attack. Ordinarily, she wouldn't run from a bear. It would only incite them to chase you, but this was one time when she couldn't afford to stand her ground and hope to intimidate the bear.

Scrambling across brush and rocks, she fought against the pain in her knee to move as fast as she could. She looked over her shoulder. The bear was running in her direction but didn't seemed to be focused on her.

Yet.

But it would notice her eventually and when it did, she had little to no chance of outrunning it, or surviving an attack.

She kept waiting for that third shot. The one that would most likely hit the bear just enough to wound it. Just enough to take it from flight to fury. From fear to pained outrage.

Enough to make it want to kill.

There had never been a time when she actually considered killing someone—until now. Doug Carroll wasn't just a bad man, he was downright evil. Who did this to people?

The fear clawed at her and she lost her footing, slipping on the dirt and rocks, going down hard on her already aching knee. Screaming, she scrambled to her feet, glancing back at the bear who was getting closer with every second.

And now, it was looking straight at her.

She couldn't outrun a bear on flat ground in perfect condition. How was she supposed to do it when she was tired, hungry, and limping?

She couldn't.

Her heart was pounding so hard her chest hurt. Or was that because she was struggling to breathe? It was hard to tell. She'd been in danger before—it was hard to live in the wilds of Alaska and not face danger, but never like this.

The growling was louder now, sounding no more than thirty, forty feet behind her. Her foot landed on a rock, twisting her ankle and she went down.

She quickly flipped over on her back, preparing herself to be attacked.

The bear was loping toward her and barely twenty feet away.

There was a desire to close her eyes, tuck into a ball, and prepare to die, but she couldn't do it. It was like she was mesmerized by the oncoming attack.

Ten feet.

A shot rang out and the bear screamed, flinging itself upright. It towered above her, over eight feet and thirteen hundred pounds of teeth and fur, with six inch claws that could disembowel her in a matter of minutes. He let out an outraged roar seemed to vibrate right through EmmaLeigh's body.

This was it. No way to run. Nowhere to hide.

*

Zoe gazed through the binoculars at the expanse below. Every once in a while, either she or Donnie would think they'd spotted something only to have a closer pass over prove it to be just rocks, trees, or shadows.

As the hours and days, along with the endless miles and disappointments, ticked by, Zoe grew more and more distressed.

This was her fault. She should have known as soon as the

bad feelings descended that she needed to set aside all the craziness in her life, get alone with the Lord, and stay there in prayer until she understood what she was being warned of.

But no, she had to let the stress and the demands and the plans so encompass her, she'd reacted with her brain instead of her spirit.

"You back there beating yourself up again?" Donnie asked.

"It's that obvious?"

"To someone who knows you, yes. And you need to stop."

She was about to reply when they heard a transmission on the radio. "Affirmative. We have located the plane."

Zoe's heart slammed against her ribs and she reached forward to grab Donnie's arm. "They found them!"

Then they heard, "Negative. No signs of life."

Zoe felt the guttural scream from deep within her heart. "No!"

*

Maryland

While canvassing the area around The Loop Bar, it was Marsha who found a couple of prostitutes willing to talk about Hayes. And they mentioned a woman named Ariella Brown.

"That ain't 'er real name, course, but don't know what that is. Just know her as Ariella." Lucy laughed, showing off her gold tooth. "She has a thing for mermaids."

Her friend, Belle, shook her head. "Ain't about mermaids. She's just thinks she's better than us a'cause she with that Hayes. As if anyone with any sense would want a man like 'em. He's dirt is what he is. I tried to tell her, he git tired of you, girl, you just going to disappear, but she don't listen."

"Do you think Ariella would talk to me?" Marsha asked.

Belle snorted. "Not that she'd want to, but if you scared

her enough, she'll do anything."

"Any idea where I might find her?"

Lucy laughed again. "Madeline's Salon. Two blocks down. She's there near every other day getting a manicure or a pedicure or new highlights."

Belle nodded as she warily glanced around to make sure no one was paying any attention to them talking to the cops. "She likes getting pampered. Facials, massages, all that fancy stuff. Makes her think she's actually made it somewhere."

Lucy was inching away, a clear sign they'd said about all they were going to risk saying. "If she ain't there, try those fancy dress shops over on Wilton. If you see that little red convertible Hayes bought for her, you'll find her somewhere close by."

Marsha called Matt who sent Gerry Otis out to help her find Ariella.

Gerry took first watch at the salon while Marsha headed over to the shopping district. A little after two, Marsha spotted a red Mustang convertible pull up and park. As soon as the bleach blond climbed out of the car, tugging at her impossibly short skirt, Marsha knew she'd found Ariella. She radioed Gerry to join her.

"Where is she?" he asked fifteen minutes later when he arrived.

"In that dress shop right there. Let her do some shopping, use up a little energy, then we'll get her when she comes out."

"It's only been maybe twenty minutes. Think she'll be in there much longer?"

Marsha shrugged. "Hard to say. If she sees plenty to try on, she'll be in there another hour. If she doesn't, she could be out in five. Why?"

"Thought I'd hit the coffee place across the street and get us something."

"Make it quick."

Sure enough, Gerry was half-way across the street with a coffee in each hand when Ariella left the salon with only one bag. She was walking quickly to her car. Marsha waved to

Gerry.

He tried to jog across to her before the Mustang roared off, but in the end, he tossed the coffees aside and ran full out, jumping into Marsha's car.

"It figures. It just figures. If she'd stayed in there just a couple more minutes."

Marsha laughed as she wove through the traffic, keeping the Mustang in view while trying not to let Ariella know she was being followed. "Maybe she's not done shopping yet."

"I hope not. I don't think Matt is going to want to hear that we didn't get our hands on Ariella because mine were full of coffee."

"No, I don't think Matt would be amused at all."

"Do you think they'll find the Lieutenant?"

"I have to believe they will, Gerry. I can't consider anything else. It would be too depressing."

*

It took a second for EmmaLeigh to realize someone was calling her name. Crab crawling backward, she moved away from the bear and finally her brain snapped into gear. Jumping to her feet, she ran, limped, skipped back toward JJ.

When she collapsed next to him, she was out of breath but forced herself to look back. The bear was running up the hill, away from both shooters.

JJ's hand fell as if the weight of the gun was too much for him to handle. "Glad to see I'm still of some value," he said softly.

She sat there, arms wrapped around her knees, breathing hard and trying to calm down. The danger was gone. She was fine. Everything was okay. She was alive. She was going to stay alive. Calm down. Breathe deep.

Burying her face in her hands, she started to cry. She hated crying—considered herself tougher than that, but at that moment, it all came crashing down on her.

Emotions overwhelmed her—fear, confusion, distrust, pain, hunger, fatigue. She wanted to curl up in a ball and disappear. Unfortunately, she knew all too well that life had to be faced head-on. Swiping at her tears, she lifted her head and looked over at JJ. "Thank you. I can't begin to tell you how much...you saved my life, Lieutenant. That bear had me."

"Nothing compared... to what you've... done for me."

"I thought you were passed out."

"Heard gunshots. Saw what Carroll was doing. Just took me... a while to get my hand to stop shaking as I aimed. Knew I couldn't kill it... but thought I might be able... to make it think twice."

"You hit him on the side of the face. That stung. It won't kill him, thankfully, but it did do the trick."

"But Carroll is right on top of us. Has us in his sights."

EmmaLeigh couldn't argue with that. "These boulders will give us some protection but he can always slide around that ledge to get us back in his sights."

"He's pinned us in."

The Lieutenant looked so defeated, she had to try and encourage him even though she felt as down as he did.

She gazed up at the ledge above them. "Here's the thing, I'm no detective, but I do know predators and this doesn't make sense."

"What?"

"He could pick us off anytime he wanted. He has the high ground. We're partially exposed. But he didn't. He hasn't. Shoot at a bear to make it charge me, yes. Spread blood and guts around us to draw predators, yes. Shoot us? No. Why not? If he wants us dead that bad, why not shoot us?"

She shook her head. "I don't think he wants to kill us. I think he wants us to die from some kind of natural causes so that there's no murder rap on him or whoever hired him."

"And it wouldn't hurt if our bodies were never found," JJ added. "Makes sense in a twisted kind of way."

"It's like torture, Lieutenant. Suffer. Know you're going to die in the end. You hold out hope. Hope comes and goes. Despair sets in. He's torturing us. And doing a right fine job of it, too." She swiped angrily at the tears still trickling down her face. "Well, now he's gone and made me mad."

JJ smiled. "Yeah, you remind me of Zoe. She's a fighter like you."

EmmaLeigh looked over at him. "This Zoe must be something special. You talk to her when you're unconscious. Just thought you should know."

"I do? What do…I say to her?"

"That you love her. And things like you're having a conversation with her. Once you said, 'Lose me? When pigs fly.'"

JJ laughed and it turned into a choking cough. "She is special. Definitely one of a kind."

"How did you meet her?"

"Chief brought her in…to assist on a child abduction case."

"Wow. She is special to be able to handle those kind of cases. So, she's a cop?"

"No. She was a crime psychic."

"Was?"

"Denounced it when she came to know the Lord."

EmmaLeigh fell silent for a few minutes and then said, "As soon as it gets dark, I'll move us further up river. We'll be fine. In the meantime, we have these." She emptied her pockets of the blueberries and he snatched a handful up like he'd never had them before.

"Eat slow," she admonished.

"What day is it?" he asked, chewing on a few berries.

She popped a couple in her mouth, letting the flavor and juice explode on her tongue. "I'm pretty sure it's Monday."

"A week. They've more than likely given up on us."

"A random hiker, a missing tourist, maybe. A cop? Two cops, in their mind, I don't think so. They're out there."

"You didn't kill Ian, did you?"

She stared at him long and hard and finally looked out

over the river. "No, Lieutenant, I didn't."

That's when she realized her rock was moving. She jumped to her feet. "Be right back."

Sure enough, she'd hooked a fish. Using a flat rock nearby, she used it to wrap the line around as she hauled it in. Granted, she felt exposed the entire time and was half expecting to hear a gunshot, but all was quiet, and she was hungry enough to risk it.

She was starting to feel confident her theory might be right on target.

It was all about torture now.

It took a little time to gather up some driftwood and start a fire and by the time she was ready to cook the fish, the sun was low in the sky, making the fire stand out even more.

No salt, pepper, lemon or tartar sauce, but she doubted either of them minded. It tasted like heaven to her and she wolfed down her half. The Lieutenant wasn't complaining either as he leaned on one elbow and shoved the fish in as fast she was.

"I've never loved fish, but right at this moment, it tastes better than steak."

She laughed, feeling better, stronger, and more optimistic. "Not that you'd turn down a good steak if someone handed you one."

JJ shrugged. "I don't know that I'd turn down anything edible right about now."

She mindlessly rubbed her sore knee as she stared at the fire.

"Tell me about Hayes," JJ asked. "Why is he doing this to you?"

Shrugging, she looked over at him. "I have no idea why, to be honest. I only went out with him a couple of times. Hard to believe that being dumped after a couple of dates would make him hate me so much, that he'd do all this to me."

"I'm thinking that I'm the target. You're just the lure to get me where he wanted me to die."

"Alaska?"

"The phone calls from Hayes. Why was he calling you?"

"To tell me that he was going to kill me. That he hated me. He sent me pictures showing that he had someone following me. I panicked and ran."

"And I think maybe that's exactly what you were supposed to do. You panic and run, he makes it look like you were a killer, I come after you. I get dead. No one looks at him. Nice and tidy."

"Why does he want you dead?"

"Now that is the million dollar question." He shifted positions, wincing as he moved."

"Let me take a look at that leg."

"There's no point. If it's better, there's nothing to do. If it's worse, there's nothing you *can* do."

She leaned over and touched his forehead. "You're still running a fever."

"At least I don't feel the cold as much."

"It's not as cold down here as it was up on the ridge but if I could, I'd dunk you in the river."

"Water's cold?"

She laughed. "You have no idea how cold. One or two degrees colder and it would be ice."

"If that doesn't break a fever, nothing will, but I think I'll pass." His voice was getting weaker. Softer. And she knew that it was effort for him to even talk now. So, she fell silent, letting him finally close his eyes and drift off.

*

Donnie sat beside her at the table, his hand on her shoulder, as the commander gave Zoe listened all the details. The crash site was found, the pilot was found, but there was no sign of anyone else. Of concern were some scattered remains and blood not far from the plane, however, it didn't appear to be human.

"You're not stopping the search, are you?"

The commander shook his head. "No, ma'am. We'll be

back out there in the morning and we're going to bring all our resources to that area, so if they're out there, trying to walk out, we'll find them."

Zoe let his words slowly sink in but this time, they didn't find a resting place. The prayers were working. She was getting her strength back, her trust back. "They are out there. I know they are."

"I understand, Miss Shefford, but please keep in mind that while we have found the crash site, we have not found them. It may take a few more days. They might be in these forests here—" he pointed on the map to an area not far from the marked crash site. "Spotting them from the air if they are in there will be difficult if not impossible."

"I hear it in your voice, Commander. You don't believe we will find them alive, do you?"

The man looked down and then back up. "Honestly? It's been a week, Miss Shefford. Even if they walked away from the crash site—as it appears they may have—they still had to contend with frigid temperatures, wild animals, raging rivers, treacherous shale fields. We have to be ready to accept whatever we may find."

Zoe stood up, shoving her chair aside. "We will find them and we will find them alive."

"I'm not attempting to crush your hopes, Miss Shefford."

Zoe picked up her purse and stepped back away from the table. "It's not about hope, Commander. It's about faith."

*

Matt left Mary Jane Skaggs, aka Ariella Brown, sitting in the conference room alone for over an hour to wear her down a bit before he finally strolled in, tossed a file folder down and pulled out a chair. "Mary Jane."

"Ariella," she replied, lifting her chin.

"Mary Jane Skaggs." He eased down into the chair, never taking his eyes off the woman. She had big blue eyes which according to her previous arrest record were colored contacts. Natural eye color was listed as hazel. She'd colored her hair blond, and was wearing more makeup than a twenty-four-year-old needed. But then, Mary Jane Skaggs had led a hard life and it showed mostly around her eyes. Unhappy sharing a two bedroom mobile home with four siblings and her parents, she'd run away from home at the age of sixteen. Actually, she tried twice while she was fifteen but the police found her both times and returned her to her mom before she'd escaped the county, much less the state. She must have figured out what she'd done wrong the first two times because the third time was the charm.

"Born in Romney, West Virginia. Mother was a waitress. Father was a mechanic."

"She was a druggie and he was a drunk." She practically snarled the words.

"Didn't much like your life, did you?"

She just glared at him before dropping her eyes to her manicure, trying to look bored but not quite pulling it off.

"Six arrests and convictions for possession and solicitation and two for shoplifting." Matt sighed for affect.

"You don't know nothin'."

"I know I've seen hundreds of girls just like you with the same story and most of them are dead now and I know a few who had worse stories that managed to climb out of the trap and make a life for themselves."

"Bully for them. If you brought me in here just to preach to me, you're wasting your time."

"And then you hook up with the less-than-human, Wendell Vernon."

"Who?"

"Wendell Vernon. You know, the man you call your boyfriend. The man who just calls you his latest until he gets bored with you and moves on to someone younger, prettier, more gullible."

"I don't know any Wendell Vernon. My *fiancé's* name is Roland Hayes. He's a very rich and powerful businessman and when he finds out you've held me like this and refused to let me call him, he's going to sue you."

Matt smiled. "Honey, you'll be lucky if he lets you live once he knows you've talked to us. Remember what happened to that poor kid at the airport? Chip Marsh?"

She looked away and he knew he'd hit a nerve. "Yes, ma'am. He'll do the same to you when he thinks you may be a liability."

"A what?"

Ignoring her question, he opened the file folder. "Did Hayes tell you how he planned to kill Lieutenant Johnson?"

"Who?"

But it was obvious she was playing with him and his concern for JJ had his temper riding just beneath his last nerve. He jerked to his feet. "Let me explain how this is going to work. My officers arrested you for soliciting."

Her body jerked. "That's a lie! I was just shopping when they grabbed me and forced me into their car!"

"That's not what they say. The word of two police officers against the word of a woman who dates a drug dealer and a killer, and has been arrested for prostitution what? Six times, Mary Jane? Now who do you think the judge is going to believe?"

"You can't do this."

"Yes, actually I can. Since you don't want to talk to me, I'm just going to call an officer now to take you down to jail. And I'm going to have them spread the word that you've been talking up a storm about good old Wendel or Hayes, or whatever you want to call him. Either way, he's going to hear you've been running your mouth and he'll put the word out for someone to shut you up in exchange for his help in getting out of jail. Someone will jump at the chance."

His hand was on the doorknob before he heard her call out. "Wait. Just wait. If I tell you anything, he's going to kill me."

Matt walked slowly back over to the table. "Talk to me."

"You don't cross Roly. He gets real mad when you do."

"Mad enough to kill?"

"Sure."

"Have you seen him kill?"

She opened her pretty little mouth but there were several hard knocks on the door and then Marsha stuck her head in. "Miss Browne's attorney is here and breathing fire."

Mary Jane, aka Ariella, smiled up at him, triumph in her eyes. "You're in trouble now."

Tuesday

Day Seven

CHAPTER 11

EmmaLeigh packed up and moved them in the wee hours of the morning. The moon gave her some light but it was barely enough and a couple of times, she stumbled and fell, dropping JJ. To his credit, all he did was grunt softly.

As the first rays of sun came up over the mountains, spreading a soft hue over the valley, she found a mound of boulders that would give them shelter on three sides and the only way Carroll could shoot at them was to cross the river—and he'd never make it—and shoot from the bank on the other side.

All in all, it was the safest she'd felt in days. She didn't even bother making a mat to stretch out on. She just sat down, leaned against a boulder and slept until the sun was high in the sky.

It was the sound of a plane engine that penetrated the dream and she mentally slapped it away because the dream was so lovely. She was with her mom and they were making Christmas dinner and she could smell the turkey and pumpkin pie.

Someone shook her hand and she groaned, desperately wanting to stay asleep.

"Emma. Wake up. Hurry."

Slowly, she opened her eyes. Back to her nightmare.

"What?"

"A plane just flew over."

She crawled to her feet, scrambling to search the sky and find it at the same time trying to figure out how to get the attention of the pilot.

It was off in the distance now and her heart sank. She should have built a fire before taking time to sleep and now it was too late.

"How close to the river was it when it passed over?"

"Quarter mile on the other side. Maybe half a mile. Hard to say for sure."

"Then they'll make another pass on this side." She looked around. "We need something to draw their attention."

"And Carroll took those flares."

"Of course." Everything was dark, silver, or nondescript. But she wasn't giving up yet. Not now when hope was surging. When there was a chance, even if it was slim.

"Your coat," JJ said in a voice so weak she almost didn't hear him. "Inside out."

It took her a moment to realize that he was right. The lining of her coat was orange. She stripped it off and turned it inside out as hope flared red hot and sun bright. They were going to be rescued. They were going to get out alive.

"You're going to be okay, Lieutenant. They'll take you straight to the hospital and pump you full of antibiotics and put a cast on that leg."

The Lieutenant gave her a weak smile. "And this time the headlines will read *Hero Detective JJ Johnson, rescued by beautiful, young heroine.* Zoe will love it."

"I'm not beautiful and I'm not young, and I'm certainly no heroine."

She glanced over at him to see that he wasn't hearing a word she said. He was unconscious again.

As she stared at him, a memory flickered and then flared. That's where she'd heard his name. He'd been one of a team that had taken down a group of terrorists led by an American general-turned-traitor. There had been an FBI Agent and a beautiful blond with long, gorgeous, curly blond hair. That had to be his Zoe. EmmaLeigh had remembered seeing all that hair during a newscast after the event and feeling so jealous. No wonder the Lieutenant loved her. Who wouldn't? She was beautiful, smart, talented, strong.

EmmaLeigh was just smart and strong. Not quite the same thing. Still she yearned for someone to love her the way the Lieutenant loved his Zoe. She sighed heavily while searching the sky for the plane's return.

It was nearly forty-five minutes before she heard the faint sound of the plane's engines in the distance. Jumping to her feet, she waited, ready to start waving her coat.

Instead of growing closer, the engines faded. Dejected, she sank to her knees. They might not get close enough to see her coat. She was going to have to come up with something they could see from far away.

A signal fire!

She began gathering branches, driftwood, twigs—anything that would burn. But when she'd gathered everything nearby, it wasn't enough. She had no choice but to go up the hill and gather from the edge of the thickets. It meant leaving the relative shelter of the boulders near the river but it was a chance she was willing to take.

A chance she had to take.

She'd gathered two bundles and was heading back down the hill with the third when she felt the burn and a split-second later, heard the report from the gun echo all around her. Even so, it took her brain another moment before she realized that her leg had collapsed under her and she was rolling down the hill.

When she came to a stop, the pain was screaming louder than she was. She glanced down, saw all the blood on her thigh, and knew that she had to move in spite of how much it hurt. Obviously, Carroll was done playing around with torture. He wanted them dead now.

She started crawling toward the boulders that would offer some protection. A bullet grazed the ground, sending a chip of rock whizzing past her ear.

Faster. Ignoring the sting of sharp rocks on her hands and jabbing into her body, she kept her eyes on the boulder closest to her, trying to see how quickly she could move with one nearly useless leg.

It only took maybe three or four minutes but felt closer to thirty or forty before she finally managed to reach the boulder and crawl behind it. She collapsed there for a moment, catching her breath, pushing the pain aside. She had to get a signal fire going now or they weren't going to get out. If Carroll was willing to shoot her on the hill, he'd be willing to shoot her behind the boulder. Nothing could stop him from just walking up and putting a bullet in each of them.

She forced herself to pile up the wood, then crawl over to the pack to get the matches she had in her purse.

The Lieutenant didn't open his eyes when he asked, "Did he hit you?"

"Yeah."

"Serious?"

"Nah. Flesh wound."

"Sure?"

"Yep."

But he must not have believed her because he opened his eyes, looked down at her leg, and frowned. "That's not good."

"It'll be fine."

"Tie it off," he said, closing his eyes again. "Slow down the bleeding."

"I will." But first she wanted to get that fire going. If there were any planes in the area, one of them would see the smoke and come running.

By the time she'd struck the first match, dizziness was creeping up on her. Fighting it off, she blew gently on the flames, willing them to surge up and catch so that she could close her eyes and pass out. No. Not pass out. She'd bleed to death if she did that.

The fire caught on the third match. By then, EmmaLeigh

was barely able to lift her head. Her arms felt like gelatin. And as she let her head ease down on the river's edge and felt the heat from the fire, she knew she'd waited too long to stop the bleeding.

*

"No. I won't do it."

Matt swung around, his face tight with anger. "I gave you an order, Marsha."

"And I'm pretending you didn't." Marsha placed both hands on the desk and leaned forward. "I understand what you're trying to do but this isn't the way to do it."

"She knows Hayes ordered the kill on Ian and that he set JJ up for that plane crash. I want her to say it. I want to be able to put that man in handcuffs and wave to him when he's found guilty."

"You think JJ's dead, don't you?"

Matt jerked to his feet and started pacing. "I don't know. No. Maybe. I just don't know anymore. I've held on to hope but it's been a week. Not one word. No sign of him."

"JJ is one of the toughest men I know, Matt Casto. If there's a way for him to make it through this, he will."

"And what if there is no way? Plane crash. Blizzard. Then Carroll. He was a sitting duck from moment one and no one knew it."

"And that gives you the right to ask us to arrest Ariella again on more false charges?"

"They aren't false. She is a prostitute."

Marsha narrowed her eyes. It might work on her kids but it didn't intimidate Matt in the least. "I went along the first time because I honestly thought an hour or two of your interrogation skills and she'd be giving you everything on a silver platter. But it didn't happen."

"Well, she's more afraid of Hayes than she is us."

"You had that one shot. It didn't work. Move on or her attorney will start filing charges so fast we won't have time to pack our desks before they toss us out of here.

Matt nearly growled. "You mean Hayes's attorney."

"Her attorney of record, Matt. You played the bluff card and came up bust. We can't try it again."

"So. . .what, Hayes gets away with killing Ian and JJ and that's it?"

"He won't get away with killing Ian and he hasn't killed JJ that we know of. Quit planning JJ's funeral."

Gerry Otis walked into the office, rapping on the open door to get their attention. "I thought you might want to know that your Amelia Browne is asking to see you."

Matt almost tripped over his own feet moving around the desk, trying to get to the door. "Did she say why?"

"No. I put her in interrogation two."

Marsha followed close on his heels as he hurried down the hallway and stepped into the room where Ariella was sitting. He stopped short. Marsha nearly slammed into the back of him.

Ariella's face was black and blue, one eye swollen shut. There were bruises on her arms and her bottom lip was covered with dried blood.

"Hayes hurt you," Matt said softly.

"You knew he would. You warned me.

Regret washed over him. "I'm sorry."

"I doubt that."

"How did you get away from him? I can't believe he just let you walk away."

She clasped her hands in her lap. "After he beat me, wanting to know what I'd told you and not believing me when I said nothing, he locked me in a room. I overheard him tell Ciero to wait until after dark and then get rid of me. And make sure no one found my body."

"How did you escape?"

"Ciero didn't even bother to check to see if I had all my keys in my purse. He's mean but he isn't all that smart. So, when he went for dinner, I sneaked out."

"But that was yesterday. Where have you been?"

"Hiding out. Making my way here. You gonna keep me safe?"

Matt pulled out a chair and sat down. "I really am sorry about this. Are you hungry? We'll get you some food."

Ariella nodded. "Real hungry."

Marsha touched Matt's shoulder. "I'll get her food. And something to drink. You stay here with her."

"And give Doc Harvey a call."

Marsha nodded and left the room.

"So are you going to protect me or not?"

Ariella looked at him through her one good eye and he saw all the pain, confusion, and distrust. He'd done this to her. He was as guilty as Hayes. And it made him sick to his stomach. "I'm going to protect you."

She stared at him a long moment, perhaps gauging whether or not he was telling her the truth or not. Finally, she sighed. "Then I'll tell you what you want to know."

"Were you the woman Ian was involved with?"

"Yeah. Rolly wanted me to seduce him. To make him think that I was in love with him."

Matt could only shake his head. "Nice guy. So Ian was at the airport that morning to meet you."

"Yeah."

"Were you there?"

Ariella shook her head. "No." She looked over at the door when it opened and a flash of fear crossed her face and then disappeared when she saw Marsha come in with a bottle of water and a can of soda.

"Food's on the way. Thought you might like one of these until then."

"Thanks." Ariella opened the soda and took two long gulps.

Marsha turned to Matt. "And I called Doc. He'll be here in a few to check out her injuries." Then she handed him a notepad and pen. "You might want this for notes."

"Thanks. Video?"

"On."

Matt clicked the pen open. He'd been so anxious to talk to Ariella he'd forgotten about recording her statements. JJ would have had his hide.

"We know Hayes planned Ian's murder but not sure why."

"There was some woman he knew that he said if he scared her, she'd run home to Alaska and he wanted this detective to go after her. But things went wrong."

"Wrong? Wrong how?"

"The detective was supposed to use a bush pilot that Doug would recommend but he got sick and wasn't there so the detective hired some other guy to fly them."

"How did Hayes find out about the last minute change?"

"Doug's been calling him from his satellite phone, telling him what's going on. He wanted to just kill the detective and the girl right off but Hayes said he wanted them to suffer as long as possible. Now that the rescue guys are getting close, Doug's gettin' nervous. Wanted Rolly to call his pilot friend to come and pick him up."

"The detective is alive?"

Ariella took another sip of the soda. "Was two days ago. But barely. He's injured real bad and Doug said if he didn't get to a doctor soon, he'd die on his own. Rolly said that was best. Then to just kill the girl with the detective's gun and make it look like the detective killed her."

"Who killed Ian?" Marsha asked.

"Ciero. He does most all the killin' Rolly wants done."

Matt leaned back in his chair. "When is Doug expecting to be picked up?"

"Two days ago."

"So, he's already out of Alaska."

Ariella shook her head. "Rolly don't have any intention of picking Doug up. Never did. He wants Doug to die out there too. That way, he don't have to pay Doug all the money he promised."

"Double-cross," Marsha said softly.

Matt rubbed his chin. "If he's been waiting two days for

a plane that isn't coming, he's knows by now that he's on his own. That is going to make him angry and desperate."

Standing up, Matt reached over and touched Ariella's hand. "I need to see the D.A. about a warrant to pick up Hayes. You stay here and eat your food. I'll be back in a little bit."

Fear jumped in Ariella's eye. "I won't have to see him, will I?"

"No. We'll make sure you are nowhere near here when we bring him in."

*

The pilot leaned forward over the yoke. "You two see that?"

"What?" Donnie turned his binoculars in the direction the pilot was pointing. It took him a minute to find the faint trace of movement in the distance. "It's smoke."

"Could be a signal fire," the pilot replied. "We need to check it out." He picked up his radio mic and called in the sighting and the location.

Zoe leaned forward. "Do you think it's them?"

"I'd say it's a fair to good chance it is." The pilot banked the plane. "If it's not the people you're looking for, it might be someone else in trouble."

"Could be just a campfire," Donnie replied.

The pilot shook his head. "Not that big, it ain't."

*

It took JJ nearly five minutes to crawl the four feet to where EmmaLeigh was laying. Then it was another few minutes to slowly pull his belt off and wrap it around her leg. By the time he tied it off, he'd pretty much used up every ounce of energy he had.

Rolling over on his back, he stared up at the blue cloudless sky above him. As long as EmmaLeigh was healthy, he held on to hope that she'd find a way to get them rescued. Now that she was slowly bleeding to death, hope was draining away.

For the first time, JJ felt the tears in the corner of his eyes. He didn't even care. He closed his eyes. *Lord, please. I know I've been stubborn, always thinking that I can do it on my own. Zoe was right. I need you every minute of every day. I don't like being helpless. I never have. But this has shown me that being helpless isn't the end of the world. That girl has gone beyond anything I could imagine and never complained. Don't let her die. You've kept us alive this long and I'm praying you plan on keeping us alive until help comes. Can I ask a favor? Could you send a plane now? Please?*

"Well, well. Looks like I won't have to kill you after all."

JJ opened his eyes to see Doug Carroll leaning over him. The man looked as bad as JJ felt—rough, dirty, hungry.

Doug smiled. "Looks like you're about done for and the girl's not far behind you."

"You won't get away with this."

"Oh, you keep telling yourself that. Perhaps it will give you some peace."

"Why?"

Doug crouched down. "I didn't care enough to ask too many questions."

"I'm going…to enjoy seeing…you in jail."

He laughed at JJ making him want to punch Doug in the face. "Never gonna happen, Johnson." He stood up. "Yes, that's a plane, but you're not going to be on it."

JJ heard the roar of the engines getting closer and closer as Doug walked away. He reached over and grabbed EmmaLeigh's ankle. "Emma." He shook her. "Emma."

But Emma didn't respond.

JJ crawled closer to the river, allowing him to watch as a bush plane landed down river. He watched as Doug walked up to the plane. But when the pilot started to climb out of the plane, Doug pulled a gun and waved him back inside.

JJ closed his eyes, accepting that it was over. Doug had won in the end.

*

Zoe had seen JJ stretched out on the ground as they flew in and her heart was in her throat. Was he still alive? Were they in time?

Donnie climbed out of the plane and then helped Zoe down. The pilot stayed in the plane, calling in their location to the State Police.

A shot rang out, hitting close enough to Donnie to make him shove Zoe to the ground. "Stay put until I get him on the run, then you get to those rocks as fast as you can."

Donnie pulled his weapon and shot at Doug who was now running into the nearby thickets. Donnie took off after him.

Zoe sprung to her feet and sprinted toward JJ. All she could do was pray over and over—please let him be alive. Please let him be alive.

She sank to her knees beside him and took his hand, feeling for a pulse. It was there but faint.

"JJ?"

He moaned softly. "Emma," he whispered.

Zoe swiped at her tears. "JJ, you're going to be okay. We're here now." But her heart knew that JJ had found someone else.

Donnie regretted his decision not to buy a pair of heavy soled hiking boots although he wasn't sure they would fare much better. The thickets were like trying to swim through a pool of spaghetti.

Gun drawn, he shoved his way through the tangle of branches, trying to find any trace of Doug Carroll. Not even a foot print could be seen.

After nearly ten minutes of searching, he decided to give up and go back to check on JJ and Zoe. He turned around.

Doug grinned at him. Then slammed him upside the head with the butt of his gun.

Convinced there was nothing she could do help JJ for the moment, Zoe crawled over to check on EmmaLeigh. Her entire leg was covered in blood. JJ's belt was high on the thigh, attempting to stem the bleeding. She tightened it and then placed her hand on EmmaLeigh's forehead. "EmmaLeigh? Can you hear me?"

EmmaLeigh groaned softly.

"My name is Zoe Shefford. We're here to take you to the hospital."

"He's hurt worse," she replied softly.

"Well, you're both going to the hospital, so don't worry about it."

EmmaLeigh's eyes fluttered open. "Are you real or am I dreaming?"

"I'm very real."

"He's out there."

"My friend is an FBI agent. He'll get him."

EmmaLeigh draped her arm over her eyes. "The fire worked?"

"Yes, it did."

A smile tugged at the corners of EmmaLeigh's mouth. "Good."

Zoe glanced back over at the plane where the pilot was on the radio. She saw the man she assumed was Doug Carroll come running out of the thicket and head for the plane. She expected Donnie to be right behind him.

But he wasn't.

Doug climbed into the plane and within minutes, the engines started up and the plane began to move. Zoe jumped to her feet.

"No!"

But it was too late. The plane taxied down the river bank and then lifted off.

"Donnie!"

Zoe ran toward the thickets, calling his name every few seconds. He finally stepped out, his head bent and she saw the blood running down the side of his face.

"Are you okay?"

Donnie nodded slowly. "He got the jump on me and hit me with his gun. I'll live but I may never live down the humiliation."

"At least you're alive."

"I saw the plane take off."

"He took it." She brushed back Donnie's hair to look closer at the wound. In spite of the blood, it was just a small cut and a large bump.

"How's JJ?"

"Not good. Burning up with fever. Barely coherent. And the girl's been shot. Looks like she lost a lot of blood. We need to get them medical attention right away."

"I'm sure help is coming," he replied as they walked back over to the rock cropping. The pilot called State Police and told them where we are."

Donnie knelt down beside EmmaLeigh while Zoe checked on JJ. He was so hot.

"Zoe? Is there anything around that we can bring water from the river?"

"You don't want to wash that wound with water from there. It could be full of bacteria."

"It's glacier water, hon. I doubt it gets much purer."

"From the looks of these fish bones, I'd say there are fish in there. Fish mean bacteria."

Donnie's head jerked up and then Zoe heard it in the distance—the distinct whomp-whomp-whomp of a helicopter. Zoe stood up and walked out away from the rocks so they could see her more easily.

Within minutes, the State Police rescue helicopter landed and two EMT's jumped out.

"Over there by the rocks. She's been shot in the leg and lost a lot of blood. He's burning with fever, his leg is splinted and there looks to be a wound on his upper thigh but I haven't taken a close look at it."

As they were examining JJ, she saw the looks they gave each other and it was enough to make her wonder if they'd made it time after all.

She felt Donnie's arm drape over her shoulders. "Don't give up hope now. He's going to make it. He's as tough as they come."

"He's so weak, Donnie."

"He's going to make it. They're going to take good care of him. We aren't going to lose him now, you'll see."

She looked up at him as the tears blurred her vision. "You promise?"

He squeezed her lightly. "I promise."

JJ was placed on a stretcher and taken to the helicopter. "We have another chopper just two minutes out," one of the officers told Donnie.

Donnie looked over at Zoe. "You go with JJ. I'll stay here with EmmaLeigh until our ride gets here."

"You sure?"

"Positive. Go."

Donnie sat down next to EmmaLeigh and brushed the hair from her face. She opened her eyes and looked up at him. "Are you an angel?" she asked softly.

"No. An FBI Agent. Close enough, I guess."

He wasn't sure what all the EMT's had done for her other than the IV, but she was already looking far better and even had a bit of color in her face.

She smiled up at him. "I remember you."

"You do?"

"Am I going to die?"

"Nope. You'll have a scar but when you tell people how you got it, they'll be like, 'Oh, you're that heroine that took on Alaska with one hand tied behind your back and saved a famous cop. Can I have your autograph?' And you'll have to fight the people off."

"I'm no hero."

Donnie squeezed her hand. "Now, that's where you're wrong. You risked everything to save my friend and I for one, will never forget that."

"Did what anyone would have done."

"No, ma'am, you did far more. Fifty, sixty years ago, I'd say you were right, but not today. Most people would have seen how the cards were stacked and left JJ to fend for himself."

"Couldn't do that."

"No, and that's what makes you a heroine." He pulled out a business card and tucked it in the pocket of her coat. "You ever need anything. Anything at all. You call me. You now have a friend for life."

"The Lieutenant is going to be okay, isn't he?"

"Thanks to you, yes."

He could have sworn he saw a bit of blush cross her cheeks.

"What about Doug Carroll. Did you get him?"

"Not yet but I told the State Police that he stole a plane and they're looking for him. He won't get far."

"He got away in a plane?"

"Yes." Donnie squeezed her hand. "And it looks like your ride to the airport is here. This is all over now."

"Will you call my brother at the lodge and let him know I'm okay? I don't know if the Lieutenant is still going to have to take me to jail or not, but at least let Adam know that I'm alive."

"I will call your brother and tell him to come pick you up at the hospital. You will definitely not be going to jail. Everyone knows you didn't kill anyone."

Donnie moved out of the way for the EMT's, but stood close by as they strapped her in on the stretcher and then he held her hand as they walked to the waiting helicopter.

Wednesday

CHAPTER 12

Zoe was still pacing the waiting room when Donnie strolled in with two coffees and a ham sandwich wrapped in plastic.

"You haven't eaten since lunch and that was now yesterday. Eat."

"They've been in there for hours, Donnie. What if he doesn't make it?"

"Stop it. He's fine. The doctors told you that they had to re-set two broken bones in his leg, clean out an infected wound on his thigh, wrap a few cracked ribs, get him on antibiotics, and treat a mild case of hypothermia. But now that he's here and getting treatment, he's going to be okay."

"I'm being foolish again, aren't I?"

Donnie urged her to sit and then pulled up a chair next to her. "You've been through hell this last week, Zoe. Some of it was you punishing yourself and yes, that was a bit foolish, but I'm not going to hold it against you. I don't think anyone would. But it's over now. JJ will pull through this with flying colors, the two of you will get married, go off on your honeymoon, and live happily ever after."

"The doctor said JJ might walk with a limp."

"If that's the worst that happens, no big deal. It's not going to interfere with his job or his life."

"He'll hate it anyway. You know how proud he is."

"I'd hate it, too but I'd hate the alternative even more. JJ may be proud but he's not unreasonable."

Zoe lifted the lid from her coffee and blew lightly across the top. She took a sip. "I forget sometimes just how proud JJ is and how easily he can be hurt. He'll forgive me for stomping on his heart, won't he?"

"I'm sure he already did. JJ may be proud, but you're stubborn and when you feel strongly about something, you're like a freight train—all this power and hard to stop. JJ knows that and he loves you anyway."

Zoe made a little sound that was part giggle, part chuckle. "He's called me stubborn a time or two. Personally, I don't know what the two of you are talking about."

"Of course not."

Zoe's cell phone rang and she dug it out of her pocket. "It's Matt."

Donnie held out his hand. "I'll talk to him."

He stood up as he connected the call. "Matt? It's Donnie. JJ's fine."

Zoe leaned back in the chair and watched Donnie as he brought Matt up to date. It was over. Everyone kept telling her that, but deep inside, she knew it wasn't. Closing her eyes, she searched for that place deep inside. *What is it, Lord? What do I need to pray about? Where is the danger?*

*

Matt hung up the phone, placed both hands on the back of the kitchen chair and hung his head.

"JJ's okay?" Paula asked as she placed Noah over her shoulder and gently patted him on the back.

She had gotten up around three-thirty to feed Noah and turned on the kitchen TV to keep her company. When she had seen the headlines that the State Police had found two of the crash victims alive, she'd run to wake Matt up.

"Critical condition but alive and expected to recover." He pulled out the chair and sank down in it, burying his face in his hands. "Donnie says that his leg is really messed up and if they're able to save it, he may have a limp the rest of his life."

"*If* they're able to save it? You mean they don't know?"

"It's pretty bad. Broken in a couple places and then a wound that got infected and the infection just spread. So they're not sure at this point."

"Then we pray. And we call everyone we know to pray. JJ losing his leg is just unacceptable." Paula moved Noah from over her shoulder to over her lap and began to rock him gently. "Give me the phone."

"It's four in the morning," he replied as he handed her the phone.

"Doesn't make any difference to the people who love JJ and Zoe." She scrolled through the phone's address book and then pushed one. It rang four times. "Rene? It's Paula Casto. They've found JJ. Yes, he's alive but in critical condition. We need everyone to pray. His leg is really messed up and they're saying he may lose it."

Matt headed for the shower while Paula made phone calls. It was only there that he allowed the tears to fall. Relief shuddered through him. His best friend was going to be coming home.

By the time he got to the office, even though it was early, everyone was there and the mood was celebratory to say the least.

Gerry was laughing as he passed Matt a Starbucks cup, slapping him on the back. "My treat this morning. Isn't this great? JJ's okay. He's alive. Told you he was the toughest dude I ever met."

Marsha nearly skipped past with a box of donuts. "Oh, ye of little faith. Eat, drink, and celebrate while we can. The Chief will shut us down as soon as he gets here."

*

Zoe sat next to JJ's bed, holding his hand, listening to the gentle beep...beep...beep that confirmed he was alive and breathing and coming back to her. His left leg was in a cast to the knee, his arm was hooked up to an IV, and his pallor was gray, but he was breathing. It looked like he'd lost twenty pounds, dark circles grooved under his eyes, and the lines on his face appeared far deeper than they had been a week ago.

A nurse stepped in, checked all the machines, and then peeled back the cover over the thigh wound and looked at it carefully before walking over to the computer in the corner and entering all the information.

"How does it look?" Zoe asked.

The nurse smiled. "It's still clean. We just need to give the antibiotics time to do their thing."

"So he could still lose it."

"It's just too soon to tell, I'm sorry."

When the nurse left and Zoe was alone with JJ again, she pressed his hand to her cheek. "I'm so sorry. This was all my fault."

He didn't move or show any sign that he'd heard her. "You've lost so much weight, we'll have to get you a different tux. We owe EmmaLeigh so much."

"Emma..." He squeezed her hand, not hard, but just enough to know that he was aware of her.

Or was he thinking it was EmmaLeigh?

"JJ?"

"Em..."

Tears sprung to her eyes. Slowly, she stood up and placed his hand across his chest. Then she turned and walked away.

*

EmmaLeigh glanced over as the door to her room opened. She expected it was another nurse or doctor to poke and prod some more.

It was her brother.

"Adam!"

"Hey, baby girl. You gave us all a bit of a scare."

"It was barely a flesh wound," she replied as he reached

over and placed a kiss on her forehead. "It was more than a flesh wound but I'm talking about being missing for a week."

"Hey, who taught me all there was to know about surviving out there?"

"I did but I wasn't sure you were listening." He pulled a chair over and sat down.

"You only repeated everything four or five times until I wanted to hit you." She noticed the dark circles under his eyes. "You really were worried."

"Well, of course I was. You're all I have, Em, and to be honest, I don't know if I could have survived what you went through."

"Yeah, you could have. You would have. And better than me. I couldn't find a Ptarmigan to save my life. But I did shoot a rabbit and caught a couple fish."

"And hauled an injured man for days, and outwitted a killer."

"Enough," she said with the wave of her hand. "I happen to know you've faced worse than I did, so quit. I'm fine. And as soon as I get out of jail, I'm coming home and not leaving again until hell freezes over, which in our part of Alaska, could happen rather quickly."

"You're not going to jail."

EmmaLeigh and her brother looked over at the voice at the door. "Agent Angel."

Donnie smiled. "Donnie Bevere, actually, but you were no shape for long introductions at the time. I hear you're doing just fine and could be released tomorrow."

"I'm not going to jail?"

Donnie hauled a chair over from the corner of the room and straddled it. "No way. You're a heroine. Keys to the city, big parade, fan clubs on twitter."

EmmaLeigh rolled her eyes. "Funny."

"So I've heard." Donnie winked at her. "But seriously, all charges have been dropped. They know you had nothing to do with any of this. You were as much a victim as JJ was."

"Can I sue, then?"

"I'd have to take my card back and withdraw all offers of future help."

"Well, never mind then." EmmaLeigh nodded toward her brother. "This is my brother Adam."

Donnie half-stood to reach across the foot of the bed and shake his hand. "Nice to meet you."

"Same here."

EmmaLeigh shifted in the bed, wincing at a twinge in her leg. "Have they found Doug yet?"

"Not yet, but they will. He won't get far."

"I meant to tell you, when I went through Carroll's bag, he had a passport with the name Roger Carlson."

Donnie sprang to his feet. "How in heaven's name did you manage to go through his stuff?"

"It was right after the plane crashed. He and the Lieutenant both were unconscious. I was trying to find out what we had in survival gear and supplies."

Donnie leaned over and kissed her forehead. "You, my dear, should come work for me."

"Yeah?"

Donnie stopped at the door and smiled back at her. "Absolutely."

"Did you hear that, Adam? Me. An FBI Agent."

"No. Not going to happen. What happened to coming back to the lodge and working for me?"

*

Donnie called Matt to give him the latest on Doug Carroll after he finished updating the Alaska State Police. The State Police assured Donnie that they would start checking airline manifests to see if Doug may have already caught a flight out of the state, or was scheduled to catch a soon-departing flight.

Taking the elevator, he tucked his cell phone in his pocket and headed for JJ's room. He'd been taking his time, trying to give Zoe time with JJ. Even though JJ was in ICU and only allowed one visitor at a time, all he had to do was flash his badge if anyone gave him any grief.

No one did.

He was surprised though to find that he was JJ's only visitor. When the nurse came in, he asked, "Did Miss Shefford just go to the cafeteria?"

"No, Sir. She said good-night and left."

"How's he doing?"

"His fever is down and he seems to be resting more comfortably."

"Great. I'll be back."

His suspicions were confirmed when he stepped outside and saw that the limo was gone. *Women.*

He called a cab to take him to the hotel and then went straight up to her room and knocked on the door. When she opened it, he could see she'd been crying.

"JJ's doing great and you're crying. I know I will never understand women, but could you help me out here?" He slid out of his jacket and tossed it over a chair.

Zoe closed the door and then walked past him to the bedroom. He followed her and found her luggage on the bed and she was obviously in the middle of packing.

"You're leaving?"

"JJ doesn't need me anymore. In fact, I think he'll be happier if I'm not here."

"Have you lost your mind or just part of it?" He leaned against the doorjamb and folded his arms across his chest.

"I was with him. And he kept calling out to EmmaLeigh. I think it's obvious he's moved on with his life. It's time I did the same."

"Yep. You've lost your mind. JJ has just spent a week in hell with a woman he didn't know and she was the only thing he could depend on to keep him alive. He still doesn't know he's been rescued or in a hospital. In his mind, he's still out there, calling out to her for food, water, help."

Zoe sank down on the bed. "He called out for her."

"And if you ask her, you'll probably find out that he spent

the last week, calling out for you."

She lifted her face, swiping at her tears. "You think?"

"Zoe, what's with you? I've never known you to be so…" He searched for the right word.

"It's my fault he's in that hospital right now. My fault that he almost died. My fault that he may lose his leg. Do you know how he's going to look at me every day of his life, knowing that I cost him his leg?"

"Okay, now you really have gone off the deep end. JJ is not going to lose his leg. I just came from the hospital. He's turned the corner. He's doing better. The fever is dropping. His wound is clean. The antibiotics have done the trick. He's improving."

He pushed off the doorjamb and walked over to squat down in front of her. "Stop blaming yourself. JJ is not going to blame you for any of this. He will tell you that it was his decision to go and it was made before you and he had your little spat."

That seemed to set her back a few feet emotionally. "He was already set to go before we had our fight?"

"According to Matt, yes. So, you see, he's not going to blame you."

"He's was going to run off to Alaska right in the middle of wedding plans from hell and leave me to deal with it all alone?"

"Yes, because that's when men do. We know you can handle it and we deal with what is thrown at us. Matt said the chief wanted Matt to go. JJ didn't want Matt to miss the birth of his son, so he took Matt's place."

"But how did Hayes know that JJ would go? I mean, if Matt was the one that was supposed to go?"

"Hayes knew JJ would never ask Matt to go so close to the birth of his son. Hence the timing of all this."

"Wow. That man is one evil dude."

"Yes, he is. Now, you need to get back to the hospital before JJ wakes up and doesn't find you there."

"I told the driver he could go home for the night."

"Then we will take a cab." He stood up and held out his hand. "Let's go, beautiful."

They were back at the hospital within half an hour. "I think I should see EmmaLeigh first if she's up for visitors. To thank her."

"I think that's a great idea." Donna led the way to her room and then waited outside while she went in.

Zoe expected EmmaLeigh to be alone, sleeping, maybe groggy, but she was none of those things, awake and animated, she was busy chatting away with a young man that held a strong family resemblance.

"Hi," EmmaLeigh sang out. "Come on in."

The young man stood up. "They just gave her another pain killer."

"That explains it," Zoe said as she unzipped her jacket. "My name is— "

"Zoe."

"Yes. How did you know? Oh, you remembered me at the rescue site."

"No, I don't remember anything about being rescued except Agent Angel."

It took Zoe a second and then she smiled. "Special Agent Donnie Bevere."

"He is special, isn't he?"

"And married with children."

EmmaLeigh waved a hand through the air. "I didn't mean special that way."

"Then how do you know my name?"

"You're kidding me, right? You're all the Lieutenant talked about. And talked to. When he was unconscious and burning with fever, he would talk to you. Something about when pigs fly."

Zoe started laughing. "That's my JJ. Look, I just wanted to stop in and thank you for all you did out there. If it wasn't for you, JJ wouldn't have made it. He owes you his life and I owe you a great deal for bringing him back to me."

"He loves you a lot."

"The feeling is mutual."

The bubbly, exuberant expression faded from EmmaLeigh's face. "How's he doing?"

"Much better. He's going to be just fine." And as the words left her mouth, Zoe felt them reverberate down deep inside. He *was* going to be fine. And they were going to be fine. The thought made her smile.

"Well, you tell him if he ever wants another tour of Alaska to call me."

Zoe laughed. "I doubt he's going to want to come back here for a very long time."

She only stayed with EmmaLeigh a few more minutes and then headed over to the ICU to see JJ. Donnie stopped at the door and placed his hand on her arm. "You tell him I said call me when you guys have a new wedding date."

"You're leaving?"

"I need to get back to work. I've wasted enough time on the two of you." He kissed her cheek. "Take care, beautiful."

"Thank you, Donnie. For everything."

"You did the same for me."

She stood and watched him walk away and as he turned the corner and disappeared from view, she pushed open the door the JJ's room. The lights were dim but nothing else had changed since she'd left a few hours earlier.

"About time you got here. I was starting to think my best girl had found someone else."

Tears filled her eyes as she walked over and took his hand. "Never. I've been so worried." The tears came with sobs now as she leaned over and let him wrap his arms around her.

"Did I dream it or were you there when they found me?"

"I was there. Donnie and I. It was our plane that got there first."

"Donnie? Where is he?"

"He just left. He said call him later. Oh, JJ. I'm so sorry."

"Nothing for you to feel sorry for. How's EmmaLeigh? Her leg wound was bleeding pretty badly."

"She's fine. I just came from her room. She's sitting up, chatting away."

"Good. She saved my life."

"I know."

"I told her she reminded me of you in some ways. Fierce, she was, protecting me from a wolf, making sure I ate, making sure Doug Carroll didn't get to me. You'd have been proud of her."

"I'm sure," she replied as she wiped away the tears.

"Did they catch Carroll?"

She shook her head as she pulled a chair closer to the bed and sat down, never letting go of his hand. "Not yet."

"You've lost weight."

"Look who's talking. If you put your tux on now, it would simply fall off."

"Then I guess I'll have to get a smaller one. We are still getting married, aren't we?"

She rested her cheek on his hand. "Oh, yes. We most certainly are."

"Good." He shifted slightly. "Have I mentioned that I love you?"

"No, what was that?"

"I love you."

"I'm sorry, I couldn't hear you."

He closed his eyes, grimacing. "The pain."

Zoe jumped to her feet. "Do you need the nurse? Are you okay?" She leaned across him to grab the call remote.

He reached up, cupped his hand around her neck and pulled her down close. "I said, I love you."

His lips met hers, soft and sweet. She dropped the remote.

THURSDAY

CHAPTER 13

Matt paced the conference room as his team gave him the updates. The bottom line was simply that Hayes had disappeared off the face of the earth and no one appeared to have any idea where he might be hiding. It was like he'd simply vanished.

"He's out there somewhere, people. Find him."

"We're trying, Donnie." Gerry twirled his pen through his fingers. "We've turned over every stone, rock, and brick in this town and nothing."

"Then let's try turning over more than rocks."

He saw all the frowns but ignored them. He wanted Hayes caught and sitting in jail awaiting trial.

"Any word on when JJ's coming home?" Marsha asked.

"Zoe said they'll be flying home Monday right after JJ is released."

Matt's cell phone rang. He dismissed the team as he answered it. "Casto."

Three minutes later, he was calling for everyone to come back. "Doug Carroll is flying in on United and due to arrive from Chicago in less than two hours. Air Marshalls were notified and are on board, keeping an eye on him. As soon as the plane starts its descent, they will take him into custody and put him in cuffs. Then they will turn him over to us at the gate. Gerry, Wayne, and Chuck, I want you with me."

"Hey!" Marsha stood up. "What about me?"

"I need you to coordinate a transport from the airport. I want top security on this. We'll come in to the back of the courthouse and straight down to the holding cells. Talk to no one. I mean no one."

"On it, boss." Marsha sprinted from the room.

"Suit up, boys. We have no idea what we may be facing."

*

Doug Carroll glanced at his watch. They'd be landing soon. He unbuckled his seatbelt and made his way to the rear of the plane to use the bathroom. He'd left a message for Hayes letting him know what time his plane was coming in. Hayes was supposed to have someone there to pick him up. Doug didn't plan on staying in town long. He'd go to Hayes's place, pick up his money, and be in the Caribbean by dinner.

As he came out of the bathroom, his way was blocked by two men. "Excuse me," he said, trying to move between them. One flashed a badge while the other body-pressed him up against the wall.

"Doug Carroll? You're under arrest."

"I'm not Doug Carroll, you fool. Look at my I.D."

"Yeah, Roger," the one Marshall replied as he snapped the cuffs shut. "We know all about it."

"You're making a mistake."

"I'm afraid the mistake was yours."

Doug's mind was spinning as they seated him in the rear of the plane, belted him in, and then took seats on either side of him. How could they possibly have found out about his alias? Unless Hayes double-crossed him. That was always a possibility. Well, Hayes just made a serious mistake because if he was going down, he was going to take Hayes with him.

*

Matt knew he and his team were drawing stares but he

didn't care. He had Carroll. And if he had Carroll, he just might be able to find out where Hayes was hiding. Excitement thrummed through him and it took everything he had not to break out laughing.

A few minutes after the last of the passengers had disembarked, he saw the Air Marshalls coming through with Doug Carroll between them. Each Marshall had a hand on him. They walked up to Matt.

"Here's your man."

"Any trouble?"

"No, but he seemed a bit confused when he realized we knew about his alias. That sort of took the wind out of his bluster."

"Thank you, guys. Appreciate this. Well, hello Doug. Welcome home."

Doug shifted his eyes. "I want a lawyer."

"Oh, I'm sure you do."

As soon as the paperwork was signed and Doug was officially in Matt's custody, they took him down the elevator to the lower level and out a back door where a police transport vehicle was waiting, engine running.

Gerry stepped over and opened the back door. "Ever been inside one of these, Carroll?"

"Treat me nice, fellas. I'm going to give you Hayes on a silver platter."

"Of course you are," Matt replied, pushing Doug forward.

The first shot cracked the glass on the door just inches from Gerry's head. He ducked, spinning and pulling his weapon. Matt stepped in front of Doug, weapon drawn, trying to figure out where the shots were coming from. One hit the bumper of the transport. Matt felt the heat of it as it passed. That was way too close.

Wayne was shouting, "The red truck," and firing towards it but Gerry was firing toward the corner of a nearby building.

Turning away from the shooter, Matt's intent was to shove Doug into the transport and shut the door.

But it was too late.

Doug was sprawled half-in and half-out of the transport, staring lifelessly up at Matt, one hole right through the middle of his forehead.

MONDAY

CHAPTER 14

"A private plane?" JJ stared up at it as he slowly climbed out of the limo. "How did this happen?"

"One of Dad's friends."

Zoe turned to Nick as he unloaded their luggage from the trunk. "Nick, how can I ever thank you? You made all this so much easier."

Nick touched the brim of his hat. "My pleasure, Miss Zoe."

She reached over and kissed him on the cheek. "If you ever need anything, you call."

He tipped his head ever so slightly. "Same goes. And I'll be wishing the two of you a blessed life."

"Thank you."

Zoe stood to the side as JJ adjusted his crutches and slowly made his way up the stairs to the plane. "This should be interesting," he muttered.

"One step at a time. The same way you'll go up the steps at your house."

He merely glared at her as he struggled up the stairs and into the plane but his mood seemed to improve greatly once he was inside.

"Wow." He sank down in one of the chairs, his hands caressing the buttery soft leather. "I want a chair like this."

"I'll keep that in mind." Zoe took the seat next to him.

"And you haven't seen anything yet."

The steward returned from stowing away JJ's crutches. "Can I get you anything to drink, Miss Zoe? Lieutenant?"

"I want a tall glass of something caffeinated."

The steward rattled off a dizzying list.

"Yeah, a Coke is fine."

"Miss Zoe?"

"Iced tea, thank you."

"We'll be having grilled Halibut with a Caesars salad and Broccoli Raab for dinner. There will be your choice of crème brulee or strawberry cheesecake for dessert."

Zoe winced. "I'm afraid the Lieutenant isn't very fond of fish."

JJ placed his hand over hers. "No, it's okay. I've developed a taste for it recently. I'm sure I'll enjoy whatever you prepare."

The steward nodded. "Very good, Sir."

"Okay, what did you do with JJ?"

JJ laughed and squeezed her hand. "He discovered that rabbit stew tasted nothing like chicken but can be good anyway."

Zoe wrinkled her nose. "Rabbit stew?"

"Don't knock it. Especially when you're freezing, starving, and in so much pain you can't see straight. Amazing how good anything hot can taste. And actually, it was just rabbit boiled in snow, so I'm not sure you can call it a stew."

"Is there anything else about this adventure you haven't told me?"

"Yep. I found out that not being in control isn't the end of the world."

Zoe's cell phone rang and she fished it out of her purse. "Hi, Dad. Yep, we're on the plane and getting ready to take off. Mom's out of the hospital? That's great. Well, how long will she be in rehab? Oh, that's not too bad, is it? So, she's doing good? Tell I love her, will you? Yep," Zoe smiled over at JJ. "He's doing just great. Okay, we'll see you tomorrow."

She closed her phone and tossed it back in her purse.

"Mom's out of the hospital and doing good. She has to go to rehab for a while, but it's all good." Zoe leaned back in her chair and looked out the window. "Everything's good."

"Well, except that our wedding venue blew up," JJ reminded her.

She merely laughed. "Even that can't hurt my mood right now. I'll be content to marry you in a barn and have the reception in a chicken coop. Just so I get to marry you."

"Okay, what did you do with my Zoe?" He reached over and kissed her nose. "So tell me about this friend of your dad's that owns this plane."

"I really don't know. Dad has a lot of friends that are wealthy because of his real estate dealings but he didn't tell me anything about the owner and I didn't care at the time."

When the steward brought their drinks, JJ asked him, "Can you tell me who owns this plane?"

The steward set the glasses down. "You don't know?"

JJ merely stared at him.

"Well, sir, this plane is owned by the Castile family."

As the steward walked away, JJ shook his head. "That doesn't tell me anything."

Zoe sighed. "Oh, it all makes sense now. The hotel room, the limo, the plane, the money. John and Miriam Castile."

JJ's brows knitted together. "It still doesn't make any sense to me."

"They own quite a few hotels in the US as well as in Europe and the Caribbean. About fifteen years ago, their daughter went missing."

"Let me guess. They called you in."

Zoe nodded, her thoughts far away. "She was just four years old at the time. The family was vacationing in Maine when she went missing. They received a ransom demand for two million dollars but after paying it, there was no further word. That's when I was called in. All the way there, I kept seeing roses but I didn't know what they meant until I arrived at their vacation residence and saw all the rose bushes."

"The gardener?"

"Yep. He collected the ransom and was just going to keep doing his job until the heat was off and then disappear."

"I'm afraid to ask."

"He couldn't bring himself to kill her, so he just dropped her off in the middle of the state park and left her there for days without food or water."

"Please tell me you found her alive."

"We did."

"*You* did."

"It's always a group effort. Tons of people, police officers, volunteers, medical personnel. I never take credit for anything as if I did it alone."

"I noticed that."

"Anyway, we found Meredith with her little pink stuffed bunny sitting at the edge of a pond—dirty, hungry, eaten up by mosquitoes and crying for her mom."

JJ lifted his head and then slowly lowered it. "So, Meredith goes home safe and sound and the Castile family is eternally grateful."

"They offered me the ransom money since it was recovered, but I refused it. They must have contacted my dad. Then again, it's always possible Dad just helped them buy land for another of their hotels and developed a friendship, hard to say."

"You miss it, don't you? Finding those lost children?"

Zoe shook her head. "I don't miss finding the ones it's too late to save. I will never miss that. It broke my heart each and every time."

"But the ones you did save. That meant something."

"It meant everything, but I couldn't save them all, JJ. I leave that in the hands of the Lord now. He knows exactly where each and every one of them are."

After dinner, JJ slept and Zoe alternated between staring out the window and watching him sleep. He was alive and he was here and they were going home. Even though it had been six days, she was still marveling that her worst fears hadn't come true.

The prayers brought him through. And some of that was through the skills and courage of EmmaLeigh MacLeod. Zoe even asked her to be a bridesmaid in the wedding. EmmaLeigh had said she'd think about it but that she really wasn't a heroine. And isn't that what most hero's say?

And just as David had asked if there was anyone from the house of Jonathan that he might bless, and just as the Castile family had asked if there were any in the house of Shefford that they might bless, so she would always look to bless the house of MacLeod.

Thank you, Father. From the bottom of my heart. I know I've thanked you about a thousand times since we found JJ, but I'm just so grateful.

Her cell phone rang and she quickly grabbed it before it woke JJ. "Shefford."

"Zoe Shefford?"

"Yes."

"This is Rachel at the Emerald House. I hope I'm not disturbing you."

"Well, I'm in a plane right now, so if we get disconnected, I may just have to call you back after we land."

"I understand. I just wanted to tell you that a bride contacted us today. It would seem her fiancé decided to marry someone else and eloped, leaving our bride with a reception that's all paid for. She read about you and your fiancé in the paper and she has requested that if you can use it, she would be honored if you would."

"I'm sorry, did you just say I can have my reception at the Emerald House?"

"She has already paid for the decorations, the catering, the band, the linens. Well, everything, you see. So, if you wish to marry in three weeks, on Saturday afternoon, it's all yours."

"In three weeks. Wow. I don't know."

She felt JJ touch her hand. He nodded at her. She whispered, "Are you sure you'll be well enough?"

"If they have to bring me in a wheelchair, I'll be well

enough."

"Okay, then. My fiancé says that three weeks is fine."

"Marvelous. If you would like to call me tomorrow, we can finalize everything."

"That would great. Thank you."

"Our pleasure."

Zoe disconnected the call. "Can you believe that? The Emerald House. And everything is set. All we have to do is show up."

"Sounds perfect to me. I'm all for a wedding where all I have to do is show up."

Zoe laughed, dropping her head to his shoulder.

Since her dad was with her mom and JJ's parents didn't like driving after dark at their age, Matt was at the airport to pick them up. He hugged JJ three times. When he came for a fourth hug, JJ put his hand up. "You do that again, I'm sending you to Alaska."

Matt backed up. "Welcome home."

"Glad to be back here."

Zoe noticed that he was handling the crutches as if he'd been doing it for years now. She smothered the smile she felt coming on.

Paula was waiting, sitting in the backseat with baby Noah. "Matt insisted on the baby coming so that you could see him the minute you got off the plane."

Grinning ear-to-ear, Matt opened the back door of the car. "JJ, meet Noah Josiah Casto."

"You named him Josiah?" JJ balanced on one crutch to get a closer look at the baby who was sound asleep. "He's a good looking boy. Takes after me."

Matt snorted.

Once everyone was in the car and headed home, JJ turned off the radio. "So, tell me what happened with Doug Carroll."

"I told you."

"Tell me again how my finest go to an airport to pick up an important prisoner and he ends up dead?"

SATURDAY

THREE WEEKS LATER

You are cordially invited to join us for a
celebration of Love as

Josiah Matthew Johnson
and
Zoe Marie Shefford

exchange vows of marriage
at four in the afternoon at
High Ridge Community Church

Reception immediately following at
The Emerald House

Officiating:

Pastor Jeff Taylor

Maid of Honor: Daria Cicala
Best Man: Matt Casto

Bridesmaid: EmmaLeigh MacLeod
Groomsman: Donnie Bevere

Flower Girl: Hannah Wooday
RingBearer: Justus Wooday

Soloist:

Beverly VanCarlo

Reading:
Psalm 23 by Paula Casto

CHAPTER 15

Zoe thought she'd be calm and serene on her wedding day. After everything she and JJ had gone through, this was a walk in the proverbial park.

She was wrong.

"Are you sure I haven't forgotten anything?" she asked Daria for the third time.

Daria calmly continued to twist Zoe's hair up and pin it with diamond flowers. "Everything has been triple checked."

"What about the flowers for the parents?"

"Confirmed and at the church. Rene called and said all the flowers arrived, they are beautiful, they are just what you ordered, and she's taking care of making sure the boutonnieres are on the men when they arrive."

"I did order them for both fathers, didn't I?"

"Yes, you did."

"Okay, what about—"

Daria leaned over Zoe's shoulder. "Everything is done and it's all going perfectly. Nothing is going to mess up and nothing is going to interfere. Relax."

Zoe took a deep breath. "I know. I know. It's all just

running through my head like water."

"Turn off the spigot."

"It's finally here, Daria. I'm actually getting married today."

"Yes, you are and it's about time."

There was a knock at the door and then Zoe's mother stuck her head in. "Is it safe to enter?"

While Denise Shefford walked a little slower and looked a little paler, there were no other visible signs of how close she'd come to dying. She seemed fully recovered although Zoe knew it would be a life-long commitment to a healthier lifestyle that would give her mom a new lease on life.

Daria waved her in. "You can help me keep her sane for a while."

"Glad to." Her mom did a sharp intake of breath. "You look stunning."

"Yeah?" Zoe smiled. "In my bathrobe? Wait until you see me in my gown."

"Look at your face, my love. You are practically shimmering. I doubt anyone will even notice the dress."

"How is that mom's always know just the right thing to say?" Daria asked.

"It's a mom thing." She walked over and picked up Zoe's bouquet of pink and yellow roses. Then she pulled something out of her pocket.

"What's that?" Zoe asked.

Her mom handed her the bouquet and then a tiny yellow ribbon. "This was a ribbon from Amy's christening gown. And this one," she pulled out a similar ribbon in pink. "was yours. I wanted to tie them together into your bouquet. I want to remind you that Amy is here with you today."

Zoe felt the tears swell up. Her twin, murdered more than twenty-five years earlier. As an adult, Zoe had brought Amy's killer to justice but it didn't lessen the missing as much as she thought it would.

"Perfect," Zoe whispered. "I do wish Amy could have been here, though."

"She is in all the ways that matter." Her mother tied the ribbons together around the stems and set it down. "Daria, I swear you are an artist with hair."

"Thank you, I aim to please."

"And as Zoe's mother, I'm going to say, I'm thrilled you got rid of the bright orange and blue hair and went with something natural looking for the wedding."

Daria touched her hair. "Actually, this is my natural color. Mud brown. Now you know why I am always coloring it."

"It's a beautiful color, don't kid yourself. You just like to stand out."

"Well, that's true. Besides, the orange clashed with the pink flowers your daughter is insisting I wear."

Zoe watched as her mother and her best friend bantered back and forth and sighed with contentment.

JJ wiped the steam from the mirror and leaning against the sink, starting to shave. His tux, altered to accommodate his recent weight loss, was hanging on his bedroom door, and the rings were in a box next to his watch so he wouldn't forget them.

He was almost done shaving when he heard Matt come in the back door. "Make me some coffee, you slacker. I thought you were going to get here half an hour ago."

"Where's Zip?" Matt yelled back at him.

"Next door. I didn't want dog hair all over my tux."

"Smart move."

"Where's the cream?"

"I might be out."

"I'll run next door and get some."

JJ finished shaving and brushed his teeth, then he turned to leave the bathroom.

"Well, well, Lieutenant. Getting ready for your wedding, I see. It's a shame you won't make it."

"Vernon." He eyed the gun in Vernon's hands and gripped his cane a bit tighter.

"I go by the name of Roland Hayes now. You are a hard man to kill, you know that?"

"So, that was all you."

"All me."

"And all because you fell on a chair and lost your eye?"

Vernon bared his teeth. "Because you sent me to prison and my daughter died while I was there and I should have been with her. She died, Lieutenant, and I wasn't there to hold her or comfort her or even to tell her I loved her."

"You sent yourself to prison, Vernon. You killed a man."

"He deserved it and if I hadn't killed him, he'd have killed me. It was self-defense."

"So you tried to prove in court but the jury didn't buy it."

"That's because you did such a good job of making me out to be scum on two legs."

"That wasn't hard." JJ knew he just had to keep Vernon talking and distracted for a few more minutes. Matt would come back and help him put this dog down once and for all.

Matt leaned against the kitchen counter, the cream in a Styrofoam cup beside him as he talked to Josh and Josh's mom. "JJ is pretty calm, I must say. I thought he'd be a bundle of nerves but he's barking out orders just like he always does."

Josh's mom, Olivia, just smiled. "There's time yet. Once he's dressed and on his way to the church, then watch out."

"Probably."

"It's a shame he has to be on crutches."

Matt shook his head. "JJ refused. So the doctor fixed up the cast so he could walk on it with a cane. Slowly, but he can walk on it. JJ said slow was fine as long as he didn't have those stupid crutches."

"They made him think of himself as weak," Olivia replied. "Men are like that."

"JJ is like that."

"That was really nice of JJ and Zoe to invite Josh and I to

the wedding."

"Well, Josh is practically JJ's adopted son at this point. Not to mention, he needs Josh to take care of Zip while they're on their honeymoon."

Olivia laughed. "We'd have come anyway. This has been a long time coming."

"That's for sure. But, it's all good and nothing is going to go wrong today. Oh, did I show you the pictures of my son?"

Come on, Matt. Where are you?

"You can't just walk into my house, kill me, and think you're going to just waltz out."

"Sure I do." Vernon pulled a syringe out of his pocket. "By the time they figure out what happened, I'll be long gone."

"With a police officer and an FBI agent in attendance. You really are crazy."

"Your cop friend went next door and I locked the door behind him so he won't be getting back in. And your FBI Agent friend is at the hotel, dealing with a flat tire, so don't go looking for him to be here any time soon."

"You still have to try and get out of here."

"All planned, Johnson. This isn't the first time I've been in your house."

As outraged as he was that Vernon had invaded his home, JJ had to push that aside. Right now, he had to figure out how to take Vernon down alone. A bum leg, ribs that still felt tender, not to mention the weight loss, and he was barely half as strong as he once was.

Vernon waved the gun. "Come on out."

JJ didn't move.

"Johnson, I'm more than happy to just shoot you where you stand."

Slowly, JJ eased away from the sink and using the cane, limped toward the bathroom door. Vernon stepped back further into the room, just out of reach. JJ had no choice but to follow and hope for an opportunity.

"Toss the cane, Johnson."

"I can't stand without it."

"Not my problem. Toss it."

JJ balanced on one leg and lifted the cane.

"Don't even think about it."

JJ tossed it aside.

"Smart man. Always knew you were a smart man."

"Too bad I couldn't say the same about you."

Vernon just grinned at him. "You know, I'm going to do something nice for you."

"Yeah? What's that, die?"

He laughed at JJ. "I'm going to take real good care of your bride while she mourns your death."

JJ clenched his fists. "You go anywhere near her, and I swear, even if it's not me, one of my friends is going to send you right to hell. And that's only if she doesn't do it herself."

"I heard that about her—that's she a bit of a spitfire. I like them that way. Like breaking them and seeing them beg."

"Yeah, I noticed that but EmmaLeigh didn't break and beg so easy, did she?"

Vernon reached out and swept JJ's good leg out from under him. JJ hit the carpet hard and grunted as his ribs protested. But before he could prepare for the attack, Vernon was on top of him and that's when JJ noticed how close the syringe was to his neck. He grabbed Vernon's hand with both of his but he was barely holding Vernon at bay. He was just too weak.

Matt whistled as he stopped to pet Zip and then closed the gate behind him as he headed back to JJ's. As he passed by JJ's bedroom window, he heard two voices and while one of them was definitely JJ, the other was not Donnie.

Dropping the cream, he bolted to the back door, only to find himself locked out.

JJ was breaking out into a cold sweat as he struggled to keep the syringe from hitting his skin. He knew it was filled with a deadly dosage of Rose and he wanted no part of it.

Gritting his teeth, he pushed against Vernon's hand while working to get his good leg in a position to help get Vernon off him.

He tried to buck, but it was like Vernon was Velcro, not even budging.

There was only one avenue left open to him but it was risky. If he took one hand away to attack Vernon's remaining eye, it might give the man the time to plunge the syringe.

Matt, where are you?

Vernon was laughing and JJ feared that Vernon was just toying with him and not fighting as hard to stick him as he could. If Vernon had more strength, JJ was in deeper trouble than he thought.

"What's the matter, Johnson? Feeling a little weak?"

"I'm just letting you wear yourself out."

Vernon laughed. "Sure you are. Well, if you're done playing."

Vernon's eye rolled back and he slumped sideways.

JJ stared up at Donnie who was holding the broken cane in his hand. "About time someone showed up."

"Matt had a hard time finding your spare key." He reached over and took the syringe from Vernon's hand and tucked the gun in his waistband. "He knew it was under a rock in the garden, he just couldn't remember which one."

JJ rolled over and then sat up. "Where is he?"

"On the phone getting some officers down here to take Vernon into custody." Donnie held out his hand, pulling JJ up so that he could sit on the bed. "You best hurry. You're going to be late."

"You broke my cane."

"Well then, it's a good thing I bought you a new one." He walked out of the room and returned a moment later with a silver-tipped cane with intricate carvings. It was a work of art.

"It's a nice cane."

"It's a *very* nice cane. If you have to use a cane, use one that has a bit of class. Now, get dressed before Zoe figures out something is wrong."

Zoe stood at the window and stared out at the limo waiting for her at the front door. "He's late."

"He'll be there." Daria leaned forward in front of the mirror and touched up her lipstick. "Matt said that they were just running a little late but that there wasn't any problem."

"He lied. Something went wrong."

"Well, if something did go wrong, it's all fixed now and they'll be there in no time."

Zoe took a deep breath. "Let's go ahead and start over to the church. We can just stay in the limo if JJ arrives at the same time."

Daria touched up Zoe's veil and then opened the door for her. "All right then. Let's go get married."

Zoe stepped out into the hall to find her father pacing. "Dad?"

He turned and his face softened. And then his eyes filled with tears. "Wow."

"Yeah?"

"Oh, yeah. And then some."

Zoe smiled and kissed his cheek. "Thanks."

"JJ is going to be awestruck."

"I hope so."

"Darling girl, he won't be able to help himself." He offered her his arm and then walked her out to the limo.

By the time they reached the church, Rene had called to let her know that the men had arrived and everything was set to proceed.

JJ leaned over his shoulder. "Did I give you the rings?"

"Yes, JJ. For the second time."

"Just checking."

Matt squeezed his shoulder.

The music started and the flower girl and ring bearer, both JJ's second cousins, started down the aisle. Then EmmaLeigh followed, escorted by Donnie. They were nearly to the front when Daria stepped out and began her slow paced walk.

Then the music changed and the double doors opened.

And she was there.

Matt leaned forward and pinched the inside of JJ's arm. "Breathe, JJ. Breathe."

It seemed to Zoe that is was all in slow motion but going by so fast, her head was swimming. All too soon, her father had lifted her veil, kissed her on the cheek, the soloist had sung, Paula had done her reading, and Pastor Jeff was asking for the rings.

He handed one to JJ.

JJ took her hand, slipping the gold band onto her finger. "Zoe, I take you to be my wife, my best friend, and my life's companion. In times of sadness, I will be your joy, in times of storms, I will be your refuge, and in times of fear, I will be your protection. For us, there is no more darkness, for the Lord is our Light. From this moment on, we are two bodies but one mind and one life. This is my vow."

Pastor Jeff handed Zoe JJ's ring and nodded.

She slipped the ring on JJ's finger. "Josiah, I take you to be my best friend, my partner, and my life's companion. In times of rain, I will be your shelter. In times of pain, I will be your comfort. And in times of cold, I will be your warmth. For us, there is no more darkness for the Lord is our Light. From this moment on, we are two bodies but one flesh and one life. This is my vow."

Then Pastor Jeff was closing his Bible with a smile. "And now, finally, I get to say the words I was starting to think I'd never say. JJ and Zoe, I now pronounce you husband and wife."

When the limo pulled up in front of Emerald House, Matt was on the phone. Zoe and JJ left him there and headed inside with the rest of the wedding party.

While they were waiting in the vestibule to be announced, JJ walked over to EmmaLeigh. He pulled her into a hug. "I just wanted to thank you again. If it wasn't for you, I wouldn't be here right now."

EmmaLeigh waved him off. "You'd have done the same."

"I would have, just not as efficiently." He grinned as she laughed. "So are you going to stay here now or go back to Alaska?"

"Actually, I've been offered a position," she glanced over at Donnie, "and I'm seriously considering it."

JJ caught the glance. "The FBI? I can see that. You'd be a real asset to them. Well, whatever you choose to do, I wish you all the best."

"Thanks, Lieutenant. Right back at ya."

JJ limped back over to Zoe and tipped her chin up, kissing her softly. "I will never get tired of doing that."

"I hope not."

The doors flung open and Matt came running in, breathing hard, eyes wide. "Hayes escaped. He had men waiting to help him."

JJ kissed Zoe's nose as he said, "Then you go find him. I'm going on my honeymoon."

"But JJ," Matt whined. "We're going to need you."

"And pigs fly."

"But—"

"No, Matt," Zoe said firmly. "Go away. He's mine for the next two weeks."

"Actually." JJ wrapped his arm around her and pulled her closer. "I'm yours forever."

Authors Note:

I hope you enjoyed reading about JJ and Zoe's latest adventure. I thought our time with them was over long ago, but I kept getting letters asking me for more of JJ and Zoe, so when a story developed in my head, I knew it was perfect for them.

If this is your first time meeting them, go back to the beginning and follow their journey from adversaries to partners.

Abduction

Obsession

Intimidation

And there may be even more adventures in store for our favorite detective and his bride. You'll have to stay tuned.

For more information on these and other books by Wanda Dyson, visit
Author Wanda Dyson - Home

And if enjoyed *Retribution*, please go to Amazon.com and leave a nice review. Thanks!

ABOUT THE AUTHOR

Wanda Dyson is the critically acclaimed author of six "high-octane" suspense novels and one "ripped from the headlines" true story which was featured on Oprah.

Wanda has a passion for reading, writing, horses, German Shepherds, and fresh vegetables from the garden. When she's not busy, she's sitting and staring at the walls of her new home in North Carolina, trying to decide what color to paint them. It's been over two years and she still hasn't decided.

Made in the USA
Monee, IL
10 June 2020

32926145R00105